THE
· RETURN TO ·
BEIRUT

THE · *RETURN TO* · *BEIRUT*

Andrée Chedid

**Translated by
Ros Schwartz**

SERPENT'S
TAIL

The translator would like to thank John Hampson for his comments and assistance.

BRITISH LIBRARY CATALOGUING IN PUBLICATION DATA

Chedid, Andrée 1920–
The return to Beirut
1. Fiction in French. Egyptian writers
1960–English texts
I. Title   II. Maison sans racines. English
843 [F]

ISBN 1-85242-149-5

First published as *La maison sans racines* by
Editions Flammarion, Paris 1985
Copyright © 1985 by Flammarion

This translation copyright © 1989 by Ros Schwartz

Typeset in 10pt Raleigh by Theatretexts

This edition first published 1989 by
Serpent's Tail, Unit 4, Blackstock Mews, London N4

Printed on acid-free paper by
Nørhaven A/S, Viborg, Denmark

'...into the profound depths of my blood I plunge, to share the burden borne by mankind and resurrect life... '
Badr Chaker Es-Sayyâb, 1926-1963

'Your house will not be an anchor but a mast.'
Kahlil Gibran, 1881-1931

To M.C. Granjon

CHAPTERS

In roman numerals:
July–August 1932

With numbers written out:
July–August 1975

In italics:
One morning in August 1975

It was nothing. Nothing but a muffled, distant noise. If it had not been for the events of the last few weeks, it would have gone unnoticed. Nobody would have dreamed it was a shot.

Kalya was not unduly worried, but she promptly returned to the window which overlooked the square.

A few seconds earlier, resting on her elbows at this observation post, she had recognized Ammal and Myriam, facing each other, slim and supple in loose yellow clothes. They had appeared at the same time from opposite sides of the square. As she had promised, Kalya would watch the young women walk towards each other to meet in the middle of the square.

Once they were together, things would happen according to plan.

But, during the few seconds when Kalya had been called back inside the room, everything had gone wrong. The two figures approaching each other in the nascent dawn had suddenly frozen. The picture had darkened. Was it a nightmare? Would they continue towards each other? Would the meeting take place?

*

Which of them has just been hit by a bullet fired from who knows where? Which of them – dressed in yellow, wearing the same clothes, the same headscarves, the same espadrilles on their feet – has just been slaughtered like some game-bird? Which of them is lying on the ground, injured, perhaps fatally?

Which of them is sitting astride her, legs and knees gripping the victim's thighs? Which of them is leaning over her friend,

1

raising her body, trying to bring her back to life? The question is almost irrelevant. This morning they are one, identical.

*

Kalya quickly shut the window overlooking the square. A square empty except for those two entwined bodies.

She raced across the living room. Odette, slumped in her mauve armchair, wearing as always her leaf-patterned dressing gown, called to her as she removed her ear plugs.

'What's happening? Where are you going?'

Kalya sped on, crying:

'I'll tell you later.'

Her aunt knew nothing, had not heard anything. Every morning, powdered and plastered with make-up, she sat for hours in her worn wing-chair. Every morning, she sipped the Turkish coffee which Slimane – the Sudanese cook who had come with her from Egypt ten years ago – served on a solid silver tray. Stuffing herself with biscuits and jam, she would mull over her memories. Slimane would sit, given his age and his countless years of service, on a fluted stool, not far from the armchair.

Kalya rushed past. Surprised at her haste, Slimane rose and followed her into the hall.

He saw her wrench open the drawer of the bowed imitation Louis XVI chest of drawers with the chipped veneer. She pulled out a revolver from under the tablemats, she stuffed the; weapon into the pocket of her cotton jumper and walked quickly towards the front door.

'Where's she going at this hour?' sighed Odette to herself, as she dunked her biscuit in the steaming coffee. 'Eccentric! My niece has always been eccentric. Not surprising that she chose such a funny profession. Photographer! The very idea!'

As Kalya set foot on the stairs, she noticed that Slimane was still behind her. He sensed danger.

'I'm coming with you.'
She turned round, begging him not to:
'No, no. Don't leave Odette. And especially not the child. She's still asleep.'

*

It seemed odd to her that Slimane was away for so long.

Odette sat up, her feet felt around in search of her red velvet slippers. Unable to find them, she gave up the idea of following her niece out onto the stairs, finished her coffee, picked up a biscuit and made her way over to the window where Kalya had stood.

Slimane would join her a few minutes later.

*

Kalya leaned against the banister. Her heart was beating enough to burst. She placed the palm of her hand over it, felt it flutter and patted her chest as if to calm her thumping heart. Like a small household pet wanting to be stroked, the muscle calmed down and she was able to set off down the stairs.

When she reached the second landing she heard light, rapid footsteps behind her.

'Sybil, what are you doing here? Go back upstairs at once.'

Convinced that her twelve-year-old granddaughter was fast asleep, as she should have been, she had not even thought to go into her room to reassure her.

'Where are you going?'

'Go back upstairs. I'll tell you all about it later.'

'I'm coming with you.'

The child persisted. Her dishevelled long blonde hair, her puffy eyelids, and her face, still blotchy with sleep, made her look wildly obstinate.

3

'Don't leave me!'

Time was short. She had to join the two women as quickly as possible. She had to walk across the square, with her revolver clearly showing, to avert any danger, to prevent any more shots before the ambulance arrived. That had also been arranged in the event of an accident.

She had to rescue what Myriam and Ammal had shared; maintain that hope which they had wanted to bring, together, to the centre of the square, where the various communities of the town would soon gather. Rescue this reunion which had been planned for days.

Sybil hurtled on down the stairs in her pyjamas, barefoot, hot on her grandmother's heels. In the entrance hall, Kalya urged:

'Go back up at once. I don't want you to follow me.'

'I won't follow you, I'll stay here. I want to see what you're doing.'

It was no time to argue.

'All right, but stay there under the porch. You'll see me if you open the door a bit. Don't come out whatever happens, do you promise?'

'Promise.'

'I'll come back here to you.'

She left her, took a few steps. Would she return? In a few moments, would she still be alive? It did not matter, not any longer. But she did fear for the child. There were moments when she bitterly regretted not having foreseen anything and having brought her to this country. She turned round once again:

'Whatever happens, you mustn't follow me. At the first sign of danger, go back up to Odette's. Promise?'

'I promise.'

*

Sybil and Kalya had arranged to meet in Lebanon, this remote

4

land of their ancestors. Each had come from a different continent, and it was almost a month since they had met, for the first time. The country was both familiar and strange. A small, delightful land which Sybil knew only from a few lines in her history or geography book, or which cropped up in the conversation of her father, Sam. She dreamed of it. Those legendary shores, those worlds of temples, gods, seas and suns – she wanted to see them, to recognize them, to be able to talk about them to her friends when she got back.

For the first time, the little girl and her grandmother were living together. It started as a time of happiness, of walks, of calm. Then the turmoil of these last few days.

For a week, the airport had been closed and the port sealed off. There was little communication between districts, and vague threats hung over the inhabitants and their town.

Sybil began to shout:

'I don't want anything to happen to you! I love you grandma!'

Never before had she called her 'grandma'. Usually she used 'Kalya', her first name. In America, where she had been brought up, her father was 'Sam' and her mother, who was Swedish, 'Inge'. Kalya ran back to hug the child:

'I love you so much. I really do.'

Sybil was astonished to feel a hard, metal object against her elbow. As she leaned over, she caught sight of the revolver. She did not have time to ask any questions. Kalya, in her white dress, was already off again.

*

The square was still empty. Under the two bodies, locked together, a sheet of blood was spreading, jagged at the edges.

From this mass rose a piercing, heart-rending cry.

Then, everything was quiet.

5

Revolver in hand, her gaze fixed on a window, then on a door, to guard against attack, against any danger, Kalya started walking.

The distance to the centre of the square seemed immense, infinite...

ONE

'Kalya! Kalya!'

Sybil, who had arrived nearly an hour before by an earlier plane was leaning on the barrier, her sailor's kit bag at her feet, waiting for the passengers from Paris. By her side stood an air hostess. Sybil raised her arms, waved and called out, then rushed down the corridor marked 'no entry'. The hostess stopped her.

'You're not allowed to do that!'

'That's my grandmother. She's seventh in the queue.'

'How do you know? You've never seen her.'

'I recognize her.'

'Before you can leave with her, I'll need to see her identification.'

'Her identification, whatever for? I tell you it's her, I'm sure it is.'

*

'You've been on at me about Lebanon for ages and now at last you're going to see it, Sybil. Even before I do!' Sam had said. 'Make sure you look after your grandmother,' Inge had added.

'After our trip, we'll come and join you.'

At Kennedy airport, the couple entrusted their daughter to the care of the air hostess. The following day, they would be flying to the Amazon. Both anthropologists, they were planning to spend two months living among a primitive tribe, to study them and make a film. Nobody would be able to contact them during their stay. They left with easy minds. Kalya, Sam's mother, was only fifty and she was overjoyed at the prospect of spending a holiday

7

with her granddaughter. Circumstances had until now kept them apart. Letters were exchanged between the grandmother and child. They had been preparing for this meeting for months.

*

Kalya had retained only fleeting impressions of this country which her son had never seen. Those summers when, having fled from the torrid heat of Egypt where her family had been established for several decades, her own grandmother, Nouza, used to take her off into the mountains. That was forty or so years ago. And yet, it was not tradition or nostalgia that bound Kalya to this country. So, why this choice? Probably, because of Sybil's insistence.

Encompassing sea, hills and mountains in a luminous effervescence, the small country was beautiful, it was true. And its inhabitants, as far as she could remember, smiled readily. Was she also trying to bring back Nouza? Nouza, now returned to the dust, whose spirit always went with her. Or Mario, her first love. No, she did not particularly wish to see him. He belonged to those teenage dreams to which one sometimes clings, as to a buoy, and which then fade, ousted by another, more real love.

In the arrivals lounge, the landing of several planes one after the other created indescribable chaos: people yelling, the dust, a jumble of suitcases, calls of greeting or complaint, the hubbub of the porters.

Kalya recognized the two waving arms and the golden sheet of hair rising with every step, gliding among the surging crowd.She turned to the woman next to her:

'The little girl waving over there, the one I told you about, that's her.'

'Sybil?'

'Yes.'

'So fair-haired! Are you sure that other girl over there, the one in the green dress with huge black eyes and dark hair, isn't your granddaughter? She looks more like you.'

Kalya had followed the child's development year in, year out, from one photo to the next, and knew her by heart. And then, above all, there was that unmistakable vitality and spirit.

'No, no, she's the blonde one. I'm certain.'

*

At the customs check, a man walks across the lane marked 'no entry', murmurs a few words to the official and picks up the suitcases.

'Madame Odette sent me. I've to take the two of you in my taxi.'

On the back seat, Sybil and Kalya hold hands, barely looking at each other, not speaking much. It takes a little while to span all that time, all that distance.

The powerful glare of the sun shrouds the city in a whitish gauze, while the wind is light and hot, carrying the smell of pine trees and the sea.

'Will I be able to swim?'

'Of course.'

The chauffeur drives at high speed, accelerates into the bends and whistles as he overtakes other vehicles, his elbow resting on the edge of the window and his hand barely touching the wheel. Stuck to the glove compartment with drawing pins, the Immaculate Conception side by side with the Sacré-Coeur. A mother-of-pearl rosary, twisted together with a necklace of blue stones to ward off the evil eye, links them together.

Kalya kisses Sybil. Her cheeks give off a smell of salt, sweat and lavender water. The car slows as it reaches the cliff road and Tewfick lets the tourists admire the view:

'Look, it's unique! Sea, mountains, all at once. There's no doubt about it, it's the most beautiful country in the world!'

9

'I knew it was,' said Sybil.

The driver studies the visitors' features in the mirror.

'Are you from here?'

'Not exactly,' said Kalya, 'my grandparents emigrated.'

'But you're still from here! We "emigrate", it's in our blood. I would have recognized you anywhere. You, and even the child.'

Here or wherever and despite intermixing and many generations Tewfick always recognizes these emigrés – by I don't know what: the flare of the nostrils, the shape of the eyes, the nape of the neck, a particular clicking of the tongue, a nod of the head. He sometimes recognizes them from a gesture born of those ancient lands, and which lives on, a vital thread, mixed with other habits, other movements.

To avoid another taxi which has just changed direction, the car swerves and brakes suddenly. Kalya and Sybil are flung together: old newspapers, magazines, apples, a jacket and a scarf piled behind the seat rain down on their shoulders.

Tewfick, livid, leaps on to the road. The other driver, jumping out of his vehicle too, is coming over, his fist raised.

Without ever coming to blows, the two men bare their teeth and curse each other. Intoxicated by the sarcastic remarks and curses and, to the great amusement of the onlookers they even go so far as to threaten each other with the revolver that each keeps hidden under his seat as is the custom.

Unaccustomed to these impromptu dramas, which do not occur in their own climes, the dumbfounded passengers huddle in the back of the car. Suddenly, they see the drivers stop. Of one accord, their quarrel ended, they slap each other on the back, offer each other congratulations and cigarettes, bow and exchange blessings.

'See you soon, may Allah be with you!

'God keep you healthy, friend!'

Involved in the most trivial incident, in every quarrel, in every reconciliation, God has just appeared centre stage. His name is bandied about at the beck and call of men, their loves and hates.

Sporting a radiant smile, Tewfick starts the car.

'Just a family argument. No need for a statement. Here, we settle everything ourselves. Everything sorts itself out in the end.'

'Everything sorts itself out in the end.' Later, Kalya will remember those words.

Kalya steps over the threshold of the old ochre building, and enters this square surrounded by closed doors and drawn shutters, this square over which hangs all the solitude of early morning. As she sets off on her slow walk, she repeats these words: 'Everything sorts itself out in the end!'

She pushes aside the thought that it is death – that of one of the two young women, or her own – that awaits her at the end. A death which will trigger another, and then another, and yet another. A spiral that nobody will be able to stop. An inevitable chain set in motion by the action of one individual.

And yet, this morning, everything was to be resolved. Perhaps it is not too late. Despite the violence of the past week, peace might still be restored.

Kalya inches her way forward, making her way towards the centre of the square. 'Don't besmirch the day until it's over.' This proverb is going round and round in her mind. She walks calmly so as not to provoke further gunshots. She moves without hurrying so as not to frighten Sybil – who is standing in her pyjamas, barefoot, clinging to the heavy hall door, and watching every move through the half open doorway.

This walk, whose outcome remains uncertain, this road of life or death, will go on for a long time. A long time. Snatches of the past, fragments of existence cling to it. Distant images, scenes closer to hand. Vestiges of ancient lands teetering towards the oceans of oblivion. Harbingers that assail her. Premonitions that she had dismissed of late. Blindly unaware or only too aware?

She steadies herself with each step. She forces herself to slow down, watching every recess of the square, fearing that at any

12

second a sniper – hidden who knows where, defending who knows what cause, or playing at being a terrorist – will shoot again at that quivering heap of yellow cloth over there, will riddle with bullets those two young women, now nothing but a mass of confused wailing. Kalya walks on, on, on...

I

What would grandma Nouza think if she could see me? If only she could see me, here, right now, holding this revolver?

'Kalya, if you want me, you'll find me in the gaming room.'

My parents set sail on the *Espria* from the port of Alexandria. They would disembark at Marseilles. Then on to the waters at Vichy, a breath of fresh air in Chamonix; later Le Touquet, Capri or Venice depending on their mood, not forgetting a final stop in Paris. They have entrusted me to my grandmother. I am just twelve. This summer of 1932 is our third summer together.

Nouza's independence taught me mine. In the mountains, at the Grand Hôtel de Solar, we live in two adjoining rooms. I come and go as I please. Anaïs, the chambermaid, who is supposed to accompany me when I go out, is more than happy to give me a free rein.

Nouza's hair and clothes are always immaculate and her face lightly made up, ready to be admired. I have never seen her in a dressing gown or négligée. Her fine, pink lips and her laughing blue eyes express her joie de vivre. Two tortoiseshell combs hold her slightly greying hair in a chignon. A neckscarf, colourful and light, is knotted around her throat to conceal the wrinkles.

Nouza always wears a jade ring and never takes off this medallion, which contains a photo of Nicolas. She always speaks of her deceased husband, several years her senior, as a thoughtful, wise old man, a little too austere for her liking.

*

'Orthodox yet schismatic,' according to the nuns at the Catholic boarding school where she was brought up, Nouza, although she is not religious, never goes anywhere without her 'icon'. A brown and gilt Virgin with a moist, expansive gaze, her skin covered in tiny cracks.

The minute she arrives, Nouza hangs the holy image on her hotel room wall. The frame, of precious wood, made according to her instructions, includes a stand for the glass filled with a thick oil on which floats a flat candle. The wick burns day and night except for the rare occasions when Nouza isn't on speaking terms with her icon, when the latter has not granted one of her wishes. On such occasions, she blows out the flame and plunges the Mother of God into darkness and disgrace for a few hours. As the glow was rarely extinguished, I concluded that my grandmother led a seemingly satisfactory existence, clouded by little anxiety, stricken by few misfortunes, punctuated with an infinite number of small pleasures which had become priceless with age and which she greeted with girlish enthusiasm despite her fifty-six years.

'Listen, Holy Madonna, this evening you've got to help me win my game of poker!'

She spoke to her aloud and I could hear her through the half-open door.

'You're not going to let Vera, that faded old windbag, or Tarek, that senile fool, or for that matter that fat lump Eugènie carry off the game!'

Nouza had difficulty accepting that generation of 'old people' as hers. Her enthusiasms were not spent, her mirror did not reflect a haggard face. Her gaze, it was true, rarely fell upon a mirror.

'I kneel down before you and pray to you every day, Holy Virgin. And remember that my gambling partners are all Catholics and that in their churches you look like I don't know what... marshmallow! With us Orthodox, it's quite the opposite, look how beautiful we make you: warm, sunny! I'm not going to bore you with things you already know, I'll simply remind you, gentle Mary, that I must win this evening. I am a widow and my resources are limited. Anaïs, Anaïs, don't forget to put the notebook, the pencil, my glasses and lipstick in my handbag.'

Switching from monologue to dialogue without a pause, Nouza hails her maid who is cleaning the bath. Greco-Maltese and without ties – neither father nor mother nor husband nor children, what a godsend! – Anaïs, buxom and anaemic-looking, torn between devotion and suppressed rage, between annoyance and irrepressible rushes of tenderness, has lived with Nouza for twenty years or so.

Inseparable the pair of them, and of the same order, they share a similar devotion to the icon.

TWO

Once again, the sea. Without tides, without spray, an exposed sea. A phosphorescent, liquid plain that sometimes grows agitated, boils and rages; and then, all of a sudden, becomes tame, absorbing even the tiniest trace of foam, and all that can be heard from the shore is a gentle lapping. Pedal boats and sailing boats appear.

The road is divided by a central reservation.

'That's a dwarf palm tree, next to the oleanders. Look at the three umbrella pines. The red tree is called a flame tree.'

Kalya remembers this vegetation, the wide lawns of Egypt, the borders of nasturtium, geraniums and baobab trees.

'Aren't the trees the same where you live, Sybil?'

'Not the same sun, or the same sea or the same people...'

'Do you think you're going to like it?'

'I like it already. I love it.'

Overlooked by developers or protected by an obstinate owner, a few fragile houses are sandwiched between apartment blocks. Pretentious, gaudy villas, with protruding balconies, disfigure whole stretches of the coast. Hotels, seaside resorts run into one another at a rapid pace. A luxury hotel imposes its presumptuous façade while, at the foot of the cliffs, lies a tight cluster of tin huts and a mass of brownish tents.

'What's that down there?'

Without replying, the driver accelerates. Sybil persists, placing her hand on his shoulder:

'Are they homes? Do people live in them?'

'It's temporary.'

The car speeds round a bend which brings them into a different landscape.

Pensive, the girl turns to her grandmother.

'Did you see?'

Cafés, casinos and restaurants with neon signs make a colourful splash along the sea front. White, red and yellow convertibles drive by, overtaking one another. Boys and girls in jeans, their hair flying in the wind. They exchange greetings.

*

Just outside the town, five armed men force the taxi to stop:

'Identity check.'

The driver holds out his documents.

'Your identity card?'

Tewfick rummages frantically in his pockets.

'Here it is. I thought I'd forgotten it.'

'You must always carry your card, you know you must. And who are they?'

'Tourists. A grandmother and her granddaughter.'

The man turns to Kalya.

'Passports?'

'I've already shown my papers.'

'Give them to him all the same,' Tewfick confirms.

A one-eyed man is leader. He has a huge wart on his top lip. He inspects both passports page by page.

'You said "a grandmother and her granddaughter"? One comes from America and the other from Europe?'

'These days, people move, people travel.'

'Those who can! But these two don't look alike.'

'That's their business.'

The four young men walk round the car, keeping the butt of their submachine guns close to their hips. As they walk past, they scratch a wing, or a door. Tewfick does not bat an eyelid.

'What are they doing with those guns?' asks Sybil who thinks it's like something in a film.

Kalya does not know what to reply. After the brief events of a few years ago, she thought that everything had settled down again. What was she dragging the child into? She suddenly feels tempted to go straight back to the airport and depart.

The man with the wart leans into the car and studies the passengers once again. He then hands back their passports with a smile and says in bad English:

'You have holiday, good holiday. Nice place here!'

The group has already stopped another car. Tewfick moves slowly off, then gathers speed. Later, he launches into a diatribe against this corrupt government, against the shambles the country is in, against the demands of uncontrolled forces.

'Who were those men?'

He spits out of the window.

'Sometimes one lot, sometimes another. They're all at it. They'll blow the country up.'

Then, trying to make up for it and reassure the visitors:

'It's nothing. It won't happen again. They're playing soldiers! It's all a lot of hot air. Hot air!'

However, he goes on muttering and shaking his head.

*

'They should be here any minute now!'

The fifth-floor landing is painted in pink gloss. Odette is dressed in a housecoat with a leafy design wearing a fuchsia-coloured turban and velvet slippers; she is standing in front of the elevator, with Slimane who is wearing a white tunic with a red belt.

Arms wide open, her words gush out:

'Kalya, my little Kalya. Forty years apart, forty years, can you believe it!'

Age, cataracts and sagging eyelids lend a poignant softness to Odette's gaze. Her skin and her kisses are scented with the fragrance of violet and amber.

'If only your uncle Farid were still alive! He was so fond of you. You were his favourite.'

Odette would like to shed a few tears and sniffs without managing it. Pulling a Kleenex from one of her pockets, she immediately abandons it in favour of a rose-point handkerchief. Burying her face in the linen square, she dabs at her fake tears and sighs. Dumbfounded by these Mediterranean excesses, Sybil stands petrified with her back to the wall.

'Venice! Oh Venice! Farid took me round in a gondola. Since the death of my beloved, I have never wanted to set foot in Europe again!'

II

In that summer of 1932, Farid decided to flee the heat of Egypt and join Nouza, his sister, in the mountains. His decisions were always whimsical and impulsive.

Tyrannical and muddleheaded, irascible and sentimental, an inveterate gambler, going from poker to baccarat, to roulette, to horse racing, showering his companion with abuse or praising him excessively, Farid moved around to suit himself, in strict keeping with family tradition or on the slippery slopes of the most outrageous fantasies.

He was the opposite of Joseph, his elder brother. At thirteen, on the death of his father, the latter found himself head of a comfortable fortune and a tribe of brothers and sisters for whom he took responsibility. In his first communion photograph, Joseph already had a solemn expression which he wore thereafter in all circumstances.

Farid's extravagant character – before he was thirty he had almost entirely squandered his inheritance – and his proverbial dissoluteness irritated Joseph, who assumed responsibility for the clan's good name. Calling one of his frequent 'family meetings' – Nouza was opposed to these and never attended – he enjoined Farid to change his behaviour. If he did not comply, then he, Joseph, would be forced to exercise his power and put him in the care of a guardian. Farid shrugged and left the country.

Joseph married the daughter of a wealthy merchant, owner of the Cairo 'Grands Magasins'. He fathered a family, prospered and became the most prominent member of his community, while his younger brother drove the length and breadth of France and Italy at the wheel of his Hispano-Suiza. Infatuated with renowned actresses, famous dancers – they could not resist his smooth talk, his heroic air and the bewitching irregularity of his features – Farid systematically rejected the matches that his family arranged for him in the hope that marriage would put a stop to his life of revelling and squandering.

Before carrying out his threats, Joseph died in a car accident. On a rainy day – so rare in those parts – driving back to the capital after visiting a rich farmer who rented land from him, his car skidded on a muddy path and overturned into the canal. Joseph, who could not swim, drowned in the sludge.

As he flitted from one casino to another, from one luxury hotel to the next, Farid was hastily recalled.

He soon took his role as eldest seriously. In keeping with his new function, he immediately married a young girl from a modest background, whom he found physically to his liking.

Odette had a greedy mouth and a sensual body, but a nonchalant gait and eyes without warmth. Harnessed to a violent and impetuous husband, who worshipped her until his last breath, her placidity enabled her to survive the many years of a life punctuated by rows and upheavals.

*

'Kalya, your uncle will be here in two days!' announced Nouza with a smile.

Farid had just cabled his sister. Later, when long-distance lines were installed – the telephone being ideally suited to his hot temperament – Farid used and abused that instrument. He would pick up the receiver on a moment's impulse, call from one continent to another at all hours, after months, or even years, of silence, and suddenly burst into the lives of his nearest and dearest at the other end of the line to announce that he was arriving the next day. Or else, to wish someone he had suddenly and affectionately remembered a happy birthday.

As he grew older, he imagined himself, not without some complacency, at the head of a huge table around which all the members of the tribe – which was becoming increasingly dispersed throughout the world – would at last be gathered. He saw himself, once the black sheep of the family, addressing a 'family meeting' to discuss the future of their offspring, condemn unseemly behaviour or disapprove a choice of profession. But times changed and this patriarchal dream was not realized.

Nouza, who rebelled against these customs and was pleased to have avoided all such authority since becoming a widow, gently laughed at her brother:

'You think we're still living in feudal times! Have you forgotten the dramas, the quarrels, the trials and the curses? The family was all that as well! You of all people should remember.'

Farid gazed at her with indulgence.

'You will never change,' he said.

It was doubtless because of her stubborn temperament, for which he had a secret fondness, that he loved Nouza more than anyone else. Unable to succeed in making her fall into line, he made up for it with Odette, his calm, docile wife, exercising his domination over her, over the servants and later over their five children.

Beneath his outward turmoil, Farid concealed a wealth of sensitivity. He compensated for his rages with emotional declarations of affection, begging forgiveness for his fits of anger, his unjust reprimands, and showering the injured party with gifts. Odette met both storms and repentance with the same serenity. Her children moved out as soon as they reached adulthood and emigrated to different countries.

During the long illness that carried him off, and which released him from both his portliness and his moods, sons and daughters gathered at his bedside. The lame cook, the old chauffeur, the Yugoslav maid and Slimane, the Sudanese, were present at the end. Nobody was able to hold back their tears.

Farid greeted death like a welcome guest whom he had ignored for too long but whose existence he had never entirely blotted out.

THREE

'Kalya, I've booked you rooms at the Grand Hôtel, they're next to each other. I don't know if they'll be the same ones.'

Would those wide corridors carpeted with strange motifs, where green dragons were entwined with blue water-lilies, still be there? Would there be those double doors of dark wood opening into huge bedrooms? Those same balconies overlooking the pine trees and the weeping willow? And on the ground floor, the same gaming room?

'I hope you won't be disappointed, there have been so many changes. Let me work it out: it's 1975 now, that's forty-three years!'

But Kalya had not come to look for memories, rather for a different place – free, neutral, a sort of no-man's land. A place that was removed from her and Sybil's everyday lives. A land rarely visited, which conjured up a few images, a few faces. Neutral surroundings for a true tête-à-tête: a confrontation with Sybil, echoing, across the years, her own confrontation with Nouza. Kalya loved those unusual encounters which make it possible to understand, and perhaps love, each other better.

She was not so much trying to recapture as to discover. To communicate with this child from another place, but also to find out, without prejudice, about this ever-elusive country; to decipher its special destiny which transcended the clichés of memory.

In Odette's living room, sofas and armchairs are draped, as if by the past, in summer covers of unbleached ticking. The taffeta curtains are held in place by matching silk cords. Persian carpets, stuffed with mothballs, are rolled up and stacked at the foot of the wall.

Sybil is unable to resist the pleasure of a long slide on the tiles which lead to the imposing verandah.

On each side of the room, locked china cabinets contain iridescent vases from Damas, milky opalines from Iran, jade statuettes and alabaster goblets. An amalgam of precious curios side by side with knick-knacks. Near a red lacquer chest of drawers, on a round table covered with a brocade tablecloth, Odette has exhibited her silverware: trays, mirrors and sweet dishes.

'Our treasures! Do you recognize them?'

Among those locked cabinets, those objects to be preserved, Kalya finds it hard to breathe. Odette's eyes become moist.

'I saved them!'

'From what?'

'From the revolution! Since Farid's death, I've been gradually selling off my jewelry to live. God bless him, he was a great lord. He gave me lots of it! In my wardrobes, I've got piles of linen. Here, there's no longer any danger, it's heaven! A calm country, the land of miracles. You've heard that expression, haven't you? That's what it's called: ' "the land of miracles.' "

On a shelf, among other portraits, those of Nouza and Farid stand out. Not long before his death, emaciated, his features drawn, he tried to adopt a flattering pose. And Nouza, leaning against the banister of a beautiful staircase – even when standing still, she seemed to be on the verge of taking off.

III

Nouza rarely released Anaïs from her duties, she always needed her to do something. She would send her to the village to fetch some medicine that she would immediately forget about, or give her a petit-point tapestry to finish. With tapestry, Nouza enjoyed creating the design and choosing wools of flamboyant colours, but then she quickly grew tired of the work. Restless and impetuous, application was not her strong point.

Nouza kept Anaïs busy with trifles out of her need for company, out of her unavowed fear of being alone. She would often ask her to bring a Turkish coffee, invite her to join her at patience, asking her to shuffle the cards and lay them out on the green baize.

Between my grandmother and myself, the door was left open.

'Are you there, Kalya?'

'I'm here.'

She would call me from time to time, content to hear a voice answering her own.

'Are you happy, my dear?'

'I'm fine, Grandma.'

A voice which broke the silence, that silence which she dreaded but in which I, on the other hand, revelled.

Anaïs, who had no life of her own, who had never had either husband or lover, experienced that summer the wildest of passions.

Henri was one of the group of young people on vacation with their parents at Solar. Whatever possessed him to fall in love with Anaïs, who was so dull and getting on in years? Over shy, would he risk with her what he dared not do elsewhere?

She believed in that love. She believed in it and became impassioned.

Before my eyes, Anaïs became a different person. Her skin grew translucent, her hips emerged from their shapelessness, her face grew radiant. I was touched, dazzled by the grace of her transformation, which made a lasting impression on me.

'The mountains work miracles. Have you noticed how well Anaïs looks?'

Was Nouza aware of the liaison? She chose to ignore it. Having experienced passion and despair, and knowing the precariousness of some love affairs, the constancy of others, she had become benevolent and even understanding towards anything to do with the turmoil of love. She became less demanding; without appearing to do so, she arranged things so that Anaïs could live her opportunity to the full. It was seventeen days of ardent and brief happiness.

Afterwards, Anaïs retreated into her old shell. Gradually she resumed her mask, her stoutness and her habits. Sometimes, her lips and her hands would tremble slightly, that was all. Other traces faded away.

As soon as they returned to Cairo, she asked for a long holiday. She wished to visit the island of Malta, her birthplace.

'I've never been there. Perhaps I've still got family there.'

'Will you come back, Anaïs?'

Never did she return. Never did she get in touch.

Never did Nouza forget her. Though she was to outlive her by a good few years.

Vulnerable from all sides, Kalya progresses slowly towards the middle of the square, as if she were following a procession. She is moving through a zone of impenetrable silence, surrounded by sleepy houses. A sinister silence, totally different from all the silences that she loved. A silence that contrasted with that of lakes, trees and mountains. A silence full of threats, which was nothing like the peaceful silence of the bedrooms of her childhood, her teens or her adulthood. A silence that was far removed from all those silences packed with images, dreams and private songs; from all those silences that are welcome, desired.

They came towards her, from the recesses of her memory, all those bedrooms. Especially the most recent, in the city, right in the heart of Paris. The waves, the throbbing of life outside beat against the windows, the turmoil was deadened by the walls. However the bricks were impregnated with the movement of the city, which seeped into that room in waves, filling it with life and rumblings. A full, dense silence, rich in hushed words. A silence like that of the body secretly rejuvenating itself.

Nothing of the sort here. It is a deathly silence which descends, like a lid, over the square. This place is stifling, enclosed by buildings five or six storeys high. Everything is shut in and torpid. It is several minutes since the cry rose from the depths of that heap of yellow cloth and then died away. Kalya heard it from up there, as she leaned out of the window for the last time. A single cry, crushed under the weight of the silence.

*

Kalya turns round to make sure that Sybil is not following her. She catches sight of her, in her floral pyjamas. In the entrance to the apartment block, the child gestures that she will not move.

Reassured, she continues walking. A journey without end. It contains all the anguish in the world, all its laments.

Around the square lives a mixed population from several different communities. Their lives have always been closely bound up. Despite the troubles, nobody dreams of moving away. But, because of the incidents that have erupted these last few days, news of which travels fast, they keep away from friends of yesterday, avoid one another. They fear a confrontation that neither desires.

Behind their closed shutters, they sleep. That was how Ammal and Myriam expected things to be. They had to take the population by surprise. That was all the inhabitants wanted – for the hostilities to cease and the different communities to be united again.

*

Childhood friends, nothing would make Ammal and Myriam enemies. Nothing. Before dawn, each was to leave her house and make her way to this reunion. Arriving respectively from east and west of the square, they were to dress identically, in that vivid colour which defied grief and mourning. They would both be holding the same yellow scarf. Their hair would be covered with shawls of the same colour, of the same material. That way they would be identical, interchangeable.

Reaching the centre of the square at the same moment, they would reach out towards each other and exchange a symbolic kiss. Then they would wave their scarves calling out loud to all those who were waiting around the square.

At that moment, look-outs posted along the route would

spread the news. It would be repeated and carried from district to district by friends in waiting.

People would come out of their houses in increasing numbers, most of them only waiting for that signal to assemble. They would gather in that place in the open air. From there, they would converge en masse towards the heart of the city. They would fill the streets, alleys, squares and boulevards with thousands of footsteps, demanding the immediate end to all acts of dissent, to all violence.

Those who wanted discord would not be able to stem this powerful human tide...

FOUR

Pausing between slides, Sybil studies the family photographs on the shelves. She finds Nouza's hairstyle, with its little waves, strange, and her short, tight, lamé dress curious. Her smiling mouth, and mischievous look remind her of Kalya:

'You look alike.'

Odette takes the portrait from her and scrutinizes it.

'You look like her too. You move in the same way. She could never sit still.'

The little girl goes off and pulls from her overnight bag the latest Pink Floyd album which her father had bought her at the airport. She goes over to the record player.

'Can I?'

'Everything here is yours,' replies Odette who has gone back to her chair.

Sybil sways and turns to the sound of the music. She runs over to Odette and pulls her out of her armchair:

'Come and dance!'

Odette lets herself be persuaded. Soon, it is Kalya's turn. The young girl pulls both of them up.

Slimane has just appeared, with his habitual tray of cups of coffee, glasses of cordial, biscuits and jams.

He is astounded at the sight of Odette trying to keep the beat.

'You too, come on!'

Sybil helps him dispose of the tray and pushes him towards the other two. He does not have time to protest.

'Odette and Kalya, take Slimane's hands.'

The circle closes and they continue the dance.

'This is crazy, utterly crazy,' mutters Odette, as the four of them caper across the room. 'This American upbringing is completely wild... Supposing one of the neighbours sees us!'

She shrugs and bursts into a laugh, which is taken up immediately by Slimane.

In the overheated atmosphere, Odette's perfume of violet and amber mingles with the smells of perspiration, mothballs, coffee, blackcurrant cordial and onions from the kitchen. The circle of dancers spins round and round. The smells from the sea and the pine trees waft into the living room with its French windows that open onto the outside world.

*

'I saw you for the first time at the Grand Hôtel. Do you remember, Kalya? You were spending the summer there with your grandmother. I had just married Farid. You were twelve, I was twenty-five. You were mad about dancing, you too!'

She lowered her voice to add:

'What about Mario, do you remember him?'

IV

Grandma Nouza had just handed me the telegram:

'Read.'

I read: 'Arriving with Odette. Your affectionate brother, Farid.'

'He'll never change. He makes up his mind on the spur of the moment and everything must be arranged. But still, I was missing him.'

*

A few days later, we were sitting there – my great-uncle, my grandmother, Odette pregnant and me – in the mirrored dining room of the Grand Hôtel.

Of medium height, constantly drawing himself up, my great-uncle paid careful attention to his appearance: shirts from Sulka, spotlessly white with his initials embroidered on the pockets, suit made of Dormeuil cloth and a Charvet tie. He got through about fifty cigarettes a day and two Havana cigars, inhaling the smoke.

From the start of the meal, when he removed his glasses with the heavy tortoise-shell frames and placed them on the table-cloth, Farid began to seethe. From snatches of phrases addressed to his wife, or to his sister, I gathered that he could not bear the fact that the hotel manager, his 'so-called friend Gabriel', had not come to greet him and give him the best table. Despite his legendary appetite, he hardly touched the hors d'oeuvre:

'Do you think this food has any taste?'

Odette shook her head in a vague manner that meant neither yes nor no. Nouza, a mocking glint in her eye, tapped her brother's arm.

'Fred, Fred...'

That was what she called him in moments of tenderness, or to let him know that she was not going to let herself be intimidated by his outbursts. It was too much for him. Not daring to turn against his sister, who he knew would give as good as she got, he began to shout at his wife again.

'It's disgusting mush! If you disagree, then say so.'

'I always agree with you, darling.'

Still trying to pick a quarrel, Farid then blamed Odette for not complaining about getting a poor table and the mediocrity of the menu. Her pink, full lips were slightly pinched while her faded brown eyes maintained the same impassive gaze. Farid raised his voice and shouted abuse at her, thundering on.

I could not take any more. I pushed back my chair and stood up.

'You can't talk to Odette like that!'

'Goodness, Kalya, what has your poor uncle done to you?'

My aunt stared at me as if I had come from outer space. Discovering to his astonishment my true nature and realizing that he could no more cross swords with me than with his sister, my great-uncle calmed down:

'You and your grandmother are not to blame, of course.'

'I'm not talking about myself, or my grandmother, but about your wife!'

Odette's hand grasped mine, forcing me to sit down again.

'Don't upset your uncle, I beg you, Kalya.'

The latter scratched his moustache, pulled a cigarette from his gold case and began to smoke it feverishly.

Odette's calm gaze, my face which I could feel burning and Nouza's knowing wink – all this made me feel inhibited. I sat down.

A few minutes later, my great-uncle beckoned the wine waiter. Like an expert, but in moderate tones, he complained that the wine tasted of the cork and asked for another bottle.

When the next course came, he questioned the freshness of the red mullet. This time, he called the head waiter.

'Spicy sauce is an old trick which hides nothing.'

'These red mullet are very fresh.'

'Very fresh! How do you know? Did you catch them yourself?'

He raised his voice. A few other guests stared at us disapprovingly. Farid lowered his voice:

'Where's the manager?'

'A business dinner... in his room.'

'Was he informed of my arrival?'

The reply was circumspect:

'Probably not.'

'Well inform him. At once.'

*

The manager did not delay in making his appearance. His bloated body ended at one extremity in tiny feet encased in shining yellow leather ankle boots; and at the other, in a round face topped by a gleaming bald head. He had a crown of bushy, white hair. He nodded as he walked.

'My friend, my friend!' he exclaimed, opening his arms to my great-uncle.

The latter leapt up from his chair. They hugged. No doubt the manager's whispered apologies were convincing as the conversation went on:

'Ah! Those Scandinavians, I know what they're like, Gabriel. Fire, that's what those women are! Fire!'

The manager now addressed the whole table in a confident voice:

'What about this menu?'

He was answered by an embarrassed silence.

'What did you think of my menu?'

'Excellent!' interrupted my great-uncle.

'I supervise the kitchens myself. I'm even going to write a cookery book. I'm a gourmet, a gastronome, as you know, Farid. You saw evidence of that earlier: the red mullet. What did you think of them?'

'Buonissimo! Excellentissimo!'

Content with these superlatives which Farid was very fond of, Gabriel made his friend sit down again and, leaning on the back of his chair:

'After dinner, come up and have coffee in my room. We'll be alone. We'll discuss "business".'

He snapped his fingers, gave him a wink which escaped nobody, and pulled from his pocket a Havana cigar which he offered Farid. Then turning to us, he said affably:

'The ladies will excuse us.'

Hesitating between the pleasures that were on offer and the patriarchal austerity which he forced himself to adopt, Farid looked from his wife to his sister to his host. The latter intervened again:

'Will you allow your husband to join me, lovely lady?'

To escape, albeit for a moment, the rages of her husband! Odette dropped her evasive air and acquiesced with a broad smile:

'You must go, darling.'

Farid took her hand, raised it to his lips, kissed it at length and, turning to me, said:

'A wife like mine is rarissima! You are only twelve, Kalya, but never forget that Odette, your aunt, is the best wife in the world. A veritable treasure!'

*

That summer, while Anaïs was consumed by the ardour of an unexpected passion, I met Mario, my first love.

Despite my young years, Nouza longed to 'introduce me to society'. One evening, she allowed me to accompany her to the ball.

'You will sit next to me. You can watch people dance.'

Beneath a pergola, tables covered with immaculate white cloths were arranged around a rectangular platform. The tables were collapsing under all the food. On the fourth side, the nine musicians in the band were tuning their instruments.

Very much in demand, gliding from one partner to the next, my grandmother had asked Anaïs to stay. She could take me back to my room if I was bored.

Between dances, Nouza looked for her glasses and enlisted my services:

'Kalya darling, my glasses, I need them. I'm lost without them.'

I found them in her bag, between the folds of a napkin or on the floor. She rarely wore them, preferring instead to make a play with her eloquent blue gaze.

To the strains of the waltz, the tango and the charleston, the dancers entered and left the floor. I was too young for a partner to think of inviting me to dance. I found it hard to keep still. I had pins and needles in my legs, I tapped the rhythm with my feet.

My great-uncle leaned towards me and murmured:

'Seven years ago, in Monte Carlo, I won first prize for the tango. You should have seen it! Not one of these puny creatures can hold a candle to me. True, my partner looked like a goddess!'

Casting a nostalgic and sympathetic look in Odette's direction, he heaved a great sigh.

'Your aunt, of course, has other qualities.'

*

The orchestra broke into a rumba. I couldn't sit still.

A pronounced love of dancing is a characteristic of the women of our family. Nouza used to tell me how my great-grandmother,

Foutine, could have been a ballerina if she had been born in a different place, in different times.

'Pity, pity, she could have danced Swan Lake!'

I met Foutine at the end of her life, she was almost ninety. I can picture her, paralysed, her hips and lower limbs deadened. Bedridden on her red divan, she would knit for hours. That seemed to help her forget the numbness of her body as she doubtless gained comfort from the sight of her quick, nimble fingers, their agility miraculously preserved.

My great-grandmother had danced a lot in her youth, at receptions given by her father, a minor governor of a Syrian province at the time of the Ottoman Empire. She grew up in the bosom of a close-knit family and developed into a lithe, supple girl, trailing a coloured chiffon handkerchief from her fingertips. Kneeling on a Smyrna rug, her mother accompanied her, drawing lively or languid sounds from a zither.

As soon as they set foot outside the house, mother and daughter hid their faces behind a veil, in keeping with the prevailing custom. I often wondered what they felt about this seclusion. My grandmother Nouza did not experience that restriction; in Egypt, the tradition of the veil was less strict and was already being questioned.

Unlike her mother, Nouza did not have a taste for dancing solo. She could only envisage dancing with a partner, deriving more pleasure from charming him than frolicking about on her own.

*

What suddenly got into me? Forgetting any shyness, casting away any inhibitions, I rushed onto the dance floor.

Nouza did not have the chance to stop me. And even if she had, it would have been no use, I was out of earshot and my grandmother, who did not possess a keen sense of discipline, would probably have let me have my way.

Carried away by the music, I threaded my way among the dancers. I was possessed by all earthly and heavenly joys. I pirouetted and twirled. I was beyond words. I was simultaneously myself and no longer myself at all! Somebody else. Happier, freer.

I found myself leaping onto the musicians' rostrum, jumping, feet together, from one empty chair to another. I finally climbed onto the banqueting table and ran its entire length, fluttering over the snowy tablecloth from which the china and cutlery had been cleared, leaving the strewn remains of a floral arrangement. A few glasses began to tinkle.

Unaware of what was going on around me, I pursued my blissful flight.

*

When the music came to an end, my legs suddenly gave way and I was out of breath. For a few seconds I remained motionless, my arms dangling. I felt embarrassed, naked.

The applause and cheers broke out immediately. I was covered in a shower of confetti.

For a long time, I suspected my great-uncle Farid, backed by my grandmother, of being behind that ovation. I promised myself that one day I would ask Odette about it.

FIVE

'I guessed everything about Mario. You were such a precocious child.'

Odette gazes at Kalya, waiting for a reply.

The latter makes an effort to remember. Mario had thick black hair, high cheekbones, the tanned complexion of a sportsman and a lot of self-confidence. He had just completed his law studies. Was he tall or of average height? Time had erased everything.

'I can barely recall...'

'Oh yes you can... Tell me...'

'There isn't much to tell.'

'I don't believe that! At our age, there's no longer anything to hide. I've got a beautiful love affair of my own to tell you about. And besides, I've kept a surprise for you.'

Odette's eyes sparkle. Her expression, once so passive, has become livelier with age, while her lips, which had been fleshy and sensual, are now shapeless and shrunken.

'Let's begin with Sybil. I've got a surprise for her too. Go into her room, I'll come and join you.'

*

Kalya arrived in time to stop the young girl from pinning on the wall photos of Travolta, West Side Story, Bob Dylan, Einstein licking an ice-cream and her parents beside a swimming pool.

She helped her put her things in the chest whose paintwork had faded and removed the broken chair. A centre light with dusty, bluish bulbs hung from the flaking ceiling. All the other

41

rooms in the apartment, neglected in favour of the living room, were gradually deteriorating.

Odette came in, carrying a shoe box which she placed in Sybil's hands.

'I'm putting you in charge of Julius.'

Petrified on his lettuce leaf, the tortoise had withdrawn his head and legs into his shell.

Sybil lay on the moth-eaten carpet which covered the part of the floor from which several boards were missing. She put Julius on her stomach, closed her eyes and held her breath. Reassured, the animal ventured slowly towards her neck. Lying on her back, the child did not flinch and continued to hold her breath. Kalya took fright and called her:

'Sybil!'

She did not reply. Kalya crouched down and called louder.

'I was playing dead so as not to frighten the tortoise. You see, now he's hiding again.'

She smiled a gently mocking smile:

'You were afraid it would devour me, weren't you?'

*

Odette went ahead of her niece as they walked through the apartment.

'Come into my room. You seemed worried about the child. Is she sick?'

'No, she's the picture of health. I don't know what got into me.'

She recalled the drive from the airport, told Odette about the argument, the shanty towns, the roadblock, the awkwardness that followed, the temptation she had felt to leave again.

'So many contrasts between...'

Odette broke in:

'Do you think there's no poverty in your country, or in hers?

42

It's better hidden, that's all. If there's a corner of paradise left on earth, it's here.'

In these few words, she dispelled all threat and danger, and taking her niece's arm, she said:

'Come and see!'

'But, a few years ago...'

Kalya reminded her of the fatal outburst which had made front page news.

'That was fifteen years ago! You saw for yourself, it didn't last. Everything works out.'

The same words came back again.

'But what was the cause, the reason?'

'You ask too many questions. You're like Myriam.'

'Myriam?'

'Mario's daughter. You'll meet her. She causes him a lot of worry. Poor man, I do feel sorry for him.'

'This country, do you really know it?'

'If your uncle could hear you, he would scold you. He wanted to have around him people and things that were straightforward! A country, Kalya, is like human beings: a storm followed by a rainbow.'

History for Odette was summed up by a few intimate scenes. Its turmoils and equilibrium were like household arguments, extreme but of no consequence. She could not imagine any other model for the conflicts of peoples and nations other than that of those marital rows that always ended in hugs and feasts.

She had just opened both her bedroom windows:

'How happy I am here! Look.'

Roofs and terraces mingled happily together under the relentless sun.

In the hall of the apartment block, in the half-open doorway, Sybil, her heart thumping, follows her grandmother's every move.

Kalya advances step by step along the never-ending path.

No obstacles to skirt. No pond, no kiosk for cover. No trees or seats in this square. Nor railings nor foliage nor bank. Nothing but a slab of asphalt, surrounded by buildings so close together that they seemed to form a surrounding wall.

*

A square. An empty space. A neglected stage, gradually lit by the first glimmers of the rising sun, like footlights. Nothing but an imaginary space. A film sequence in which the vital scene, repeated several times, is obsessive like a chorus. Slow motion, breaking down the images and the gestures so that they impress and engrave themselves on the minds of the spectators. A trailer, repeated on the television screen, seen simultaneously by millions of people.

This place, a tragic premonition, which could only exist in the imagination!

And yet it is real. It exists. With each step, Kalya feels the firmness of the ground. In her heart, the wail of Ammal or Myriam, of Myriam or Ammal, echoes endlessly.

It is definitely her, Kalya, in her white dress, her loose-knit cotton jumper; she recognizes its texture, she can feel the silky suppleness of the skirt around her thighs and knees. She, Kalya, recently arrived with her granddaughter from beyond the seas.

Suddenly both plunged into, linked to this conflict which was so distant and at the same time so close.

All this is true. It is quite clearly a pistol that she is holding, gripping its rough butt in the palm of her hand. It is quite clearly the trigger, whose safety-catch she has pushed back, that she can feel her index finger around.

Almost in spite of herself, Kalya follows an indelible thread which comes and goes, from Sybil to herself, and further on to the two young women so dangerously exposed...

SIX

Odette looks downcast as she begins to talk about leaving Egypt:

'It wasn't easy to abandon everything. But, after all, your uncle's resting place is here, in the land of his ancestors. The older I get, the more I put down roots. What about you, Kalya?'

'I don't think I do, no.'

What are roots? Distant ties or ties that are woven through life? The ties of a rarely visited ancestral land or those of a neighbouring land where one spent one's childhood, or are they those of a city where one has lived longest? And, indeed, had not Kalya chosen to uproot herself? Had she not wished to graft those different roots and sensibilities onto one another? A hybrid, why not? She revelled in that crossbreeding which broadened her outlook and made her receptive to other cultures.

'Why did you return here with the child? Why?'

Odette can only imagine one type of 'emigrant': those who left their native land long ago to flee starvation or the sporadic struggles between different communities, or to 'make their fortune'. From father to son, such people perpetuate a nostalgia for their small homeland which is more and more a product of their imagination, and painted ever rosier. Falteringly – tender, balmy, radiant under its cloak of sunlight – this land is recalled during a meal of dishes from home, or in the slightly drawling tones of travellers who have come from there; or again among the yellowing photographs scattered across the table after the meal.

'That is uncle Selim, Nouza's grandfather, with his wife, aunt Hind. That one is Mitry, the cousin who was a poet, in short trousers. Now him, wait, let me think... Ah! Yes, Ghassan, another uncle who settled in Buenos Aires, owner of the largest calico factory. And that's Chafika, she was a great beauty.'

On other occasions, it is a photo of a landscape which moves them. A snowy mountain peak studded with a few cedar trees; a stretch of phosphorescent sea bordered by an iridescent beach, with its faded red parasols and its wide blue huts. Or again the photo of a town or village, 'cradle of the family', clinging to a hillside covered with olive trees. At first glance, such a place could be any village anywhere in the Mediterranean, but the simple fact of naming it, thinking about it, and touching that stained square of paper aroused in each of them an emotional feeling of sweet belonging.

The first generation expatriate returned to his native land to find a wife, to have a mausoleum built for some future sumptuous funeral. In his village, he held a privileged position which was maintained by a continuous correspondence and the regular sending of money to those of his family who remained behind. Those customs died away with the next generation.

*

Odette repeats her question:

'Why here? Why here?'

There were numerous reasons for that decision. The child's repeated requests, the desire to meet outside the borders of their everyday lives.

Also out of affection. Affection for this narrow land which can be crossed in a single day, this tenacious and fragile land. For happy memories of welcomes, a concert of voices. For Nouza whose beautiful, expressive face appears, now and again, in these warm landscapes.

'For Nouza. To get to know and love this country better. For Sybil.'

47

'Mitry would have been able to explain everything to you. Pity he's no longer with us. He knew our regions well, their history, their beliefs... In those days, nobody listened to him. We weren't interested in those things. Do you remember Mitry?'

V

That summer, a week after my great-uncle's departure, which had been as untimely as his arrival, Mitry came to join us at the Grand Hôtel. On his return to Egypt, Farid had found him looking pale and worn out and had sent him to us with a letter for Odette recommending that she settle all the bills of her 'very dear cousin's' stay.

An orphan and penniless, Mitry had, with Nouza's consent, always lived with my grandfather Nicolas. With his shuffling walk, his timid gestures and his low voice, he grew old in their shadow. Despite his reticence, he was to make a profound mark on their lives.

Cousin Mitry suffered from chronic eczema which covered his body in red blotches. Fragments of dry skin peeled off his face and neck and fell in flakes or dust on his shoulders and the inside of his jacket. With a faint, apologetic smile, he would furtively dust himself down, while we pretended not to notice. In public, he wore brown cotton gloves, to conceal his hands.

Silent and gentle, everything about Mitry displeased Farid. What was more, 'he wrote'! Not only letters, but for his own enjoyment:

'A poet!'

The height of insanity! The family became aware of it from a few purple ink stains on his fingers, from that bump on his middle finger. His inability to make money, to chase after the fairer sex, to take his place in society made my uncle's judgement harsh and relentless. In his opinion, this cousin, was destined for mediocrity, and possessed the brain of a child – unlikely to develop. It had taken all the firmness of his brother-in-law Nicolas – an older man whose wisdom and prosperity impressed him – for Farid to refrain from taunting Mitry and his secret garden.

*

Full of contradictions, my great-uncle had a generous enough heart to take under his wing those whose tastes, character and interests were diametrically opposed to his own. From time to time, he worried about his cousin's state of health.

This concern is what had just granted Mitry this stay in the mountains; a trip that he would gladly have done without. He dreaded travelling, only feeling safe among his books, in his den of a room, nestling on the mezzanine with its shutters half-closed. In his cell, he accumulated books of all sorts which Farid never had the curiosity to open. True, Mitry avoided bringing anybody into his room which he kept scrupulously clean. My grandmother, who doubted the virility of a man who engaged in domestic chores, sometimes grew exasperated with him, but she let him have his way under orders from Nicolas, her husband. She had to restrain herself from pushing Anaïs into Mitry's room to make his bed, remove his dirty washing and dust the corners.

Among his few friends, cousin Mitry had gained a reputation as a scholar, but he kept quiet about his main interest: poetry. He wrote down countless poems in thin school notebooks, covering the pages in his precise handwriting with ornate capital letters and no deletions. Then he piled up all these sheets, which he would never have dreamed of having published, in cardboard boxes which he slipped under his bed.

One afternoon, he told me about them, in hushed tones. No doubt because I was only a child and he was not afraid of what I might think.

Later, he invited me into his room. The walls were covered in wallpaper with a pattern of brownish ferns. The curtains were drawn. I sat on a low stool on which there was a cushion made from damask cloth. Standing in front of me, Mitry read a piece he had written for me. I remember it as being rather sentimental, harping on the same old theme. On the other hand, I have a very vivid memory of his green eyes, the colour of water, which grew lighter and lighter as he read, of his features growing younger, of those red blotches which seemed to fade.

As he read, carried away by his own voice, everything around us became lighter. The room grew wings. Tinged by a soft light which filtered through the thickness of the drapes, the furniture and the walls seemed to be kindled by the ardour with which he uttered his words. Words of the utmost banality to which I almost fell captive.

My affection for Mitry soared. But from now on, I was to doubt the relation between the happiness one feels in one's own imagination and the consequences of such happiness.

He gave me the poem.

'It's for you. Don't ever talk about it.'

Once he came back down to earth again, did he judge himself frankly? Or rather would his natural modesty, even if he had been talented, have kept him in obscurity?

I kept the poem, more precious to me than the words it contained.

SEVEN

'I've got all his notebooks,' said Odette. 'Mitry entrusted them to me before he died. I left his books, he had too many.'

Mitry and Odette had known each other more intimately, more deeply than Kalya realized.

'Mitry was interested in the history of our communities. Although he was Orthodox, it was he who explained the Maronite liturgy to me. Farid had given his consent for our sons to be brought up according to my religion. Your uncle was a believer but he did not practise. Except during his illness, then he came with me to church. As one grows older, one realizes that religion is important, doesn't one? I go to mass every morning, it's lucky that the Chapel of the Brothers is just around the corner. What about you, are you at least a believer?'

'I couldn't say. I'm more an agnostic.'

'What's an "agnostic"? Yet another religion?'

'Not exactly.'

'You're not an atheist, though?'

'Not that either.'

'Here, religion dominates everything. It affects our whole lives.'

'Belief is a private matter.'

'If that's the way you think, you're in the wrong country, among the wrong people, in the wrong land!'

VI

'What does Orthodox mean?'

There was nothing deeply religious about Nouza, she got into a muddle with the principles, dogmas, festivals and ceremonies of our various communities. Ecumenical before it became fashionable, she avoided giving me any explanations:

'You, my little granddaughter, are both Catholic and Orthodox, what difference does it make? All paths lead to the good Lord.'

'Do you believe in the good Lord, Grandma?'

I was pushing things too far. Would she scold me? My question revealed an unusual scepticism which she did not wish to encourage. By way of reply, she pointed at the icon. Above the short flame, shone the face of her all-powerful and graceful companion.

'There's my answer: the Mother of God never leaves my side!'

Nouza joined her thumbs, first and middle fingers, and crossed herself three times in accordance with her personal litany. She invited me to do likewise. As the little wick was almost burnt out, she asked me to replace the flat candle floating on the paraffin oil. Through this ritual, which gave her succour throughout her long life and which she asked me, during our holidays, to enact in her stead, she thought I would become attached to the mysteries of the faith without too many questions.

While I did this, I would admire the contours of the drawing, the shading of the colours and the icon's expression which was both humble and sovereign. Though I allowed myself to be enchanted by so much beauty, I remained impervious to any religious fervour.

My grandmother's religious practice was restricted to this

order, to the annual visit to the cemetery where her husband lay and to the Easter meal when Bishop Anastase was her guest. He wore a tall stiff headdress. His never-ending body was clad in a dark, silky cassock. He had eyes the colour of coals and a splendid tapering beard.

On a chain around his neck, the bishop wore an amethyst cross, a present from his congregation. After blessing every room in the house with a palm branch dipped in holy water, he held out his hand for us to kiss the ring that held a large purple stone.

After the meal, he would smoke Gianaclis cigarettes in the company of his hostess who always had some in stock. Since the death of Nicolas, who had tried in vain to make her give up the habit, Nouza abandoned herself freely to this pleasure.

Constantin the cook, who deplored my grandmother's violation of his territory, her plentiful advice and suggestions, would appear at the end of the meal. In a white jacket, his hands crossed over his fat stomach, he received the congratulations of the prelate to whose flock he belonged. Then it was his turn to bow and kiss the ring.

*

'And did grandfather Nicolas believe in God?'

I returned to the attack! Such obstinacy displeased Nouza who shook her head and closed the conversation:

'He was an educated man.'

Her reply reinforced my suspicions. Amidst this multitude of religions, with all their ramifications, each vouching to speak the sole truth, each excluding all others, how did God cope?

'God is infinite, isn't he? God is for all men? God is without hatred, isn't he? God is goodness itself? Otherwise God wouldn't be God, would he, Grandma?'

I must have sounded pathetic, the problem overwhelmed me. I clung to her arm.

'Explain God to me, Grandma!'

Relieving herself of all responsibility to answer such thorny questions, freeing herself from all concern, Nouza left me standing there and went to her room. For a few hours, our communicating door remained closed. Through the partition, I could hear her discussing her choice of clothes with Anaïs.

'Shall I wear the long mauve dress or the short lamé one?'

Then she would wonder which earrings best matched her clothes.

*

There was still cousin Mitry left to help me. As self-effacing as Farid was loud, he kept out of the way during the day. He only joined the three of us at mealtimes.

One morning, in the corridors of the Grand Hôtel, I approached him with my doubts. He did not dismiss me, quite the opposite. He was happy to initiate me into knowledge which his closest relatives did not possess, into questions which they did not even know existed.

Mitry told me of the arguments over Christ which had bloodied the past, of the Islamic quarrels which had torn it apart. A history of schisms and reconciliations, of conquests, humiliations, blood and tears. Far from his library, he knew its contents by heart.

We went for a walk in the pine woods near the hotel. In his footsteps, I traced the paths of rifts and unions, of battles, of retractions, truces, of massacres and of tears.

'Man is fascinated by death, it's strange.'

To make up for the bleakness of what he was telling me, Mitry picked up a pine cone lying at the foot of a tree and hit it with a stone till the kernels fell out. Then he offered me the nuts in the palm of his gloved hand.

'I shouldn't be telling you all this. It's too much at your age.'

'You must tell me everything, everything.'

Seeing I was so determined, he proceeded. He tried to unravel the threads within these convolutions, to find simple words to describe the stormy, complicated arguments about the succession of the Prophet, around the dogma of the Trinity which divided peoples to the point of hatred. Should one be a partisan of Ali, cousin and son-in-law of the prophet Muhammad, or should one be faithful to the Caliph, his successor chosen by consensus? Should Christ be attributed one or two natures, one or two wills? Should one be Unicist, Monothelite, Nestorian, Chalcedonian or Monophysite? These disputes led to murderous struggles, to massacres and to deadly fury.

Mitry continued:

'Even today, in this country, there are fourteen ways of being a believer, a monotheist and a son of Abraham! Isn't it too complicated for you? You are only a child, Kalya.'

'Go on, I want to know it all.'

He carried on, from time to time softening the horrors of History by pointing out a chain of mountains, a leafy valley fanning out between two stark cliffs, by teaching me to love the light, to take deep breaths, to listen to the flowing of the stream, to give thanks for all the different blues of the sky and for a day of peace:

'It is fragile. Every day of peace is a miracle. Never forget that thought. Wherever you are, in the depths of your sadness, it will help you smile.'

He gathered for me some tufts of grass in the hollow of a rock, picked a sweet-smelling leaf from a bushy clump.

Then he carried on where he had left off. I had never before found him so captivating. Never again would he be so eloquent. He told me of those bloody dawns, those internal struggles, the destruction and the massacres; described those ascetic warriors and fanatics of every kind. 'In short,' he concluded, 'on this tiny surface, everything has happened: the best and the worst! A remarkable little land, but dangerous.' I could not take my eyes off him.

'Remarkable or dangerous,' he continued, 'depending on what we make of it!'

'Do you believe in God, cousin Mitry?'

He thought, and scratched his forehead. The flakes of blistered skin caused by his eczema fell in a fine dust on his eyebrows. He pulled a large handkerchief out of his pocket and dabbed his face, blinking.

'I believe in God.'

He had made his choice. Unable to live without a thirst for perfection and an ultimate purpose, he took his place, deliberately and humbly, within the faith of his ancestors. I admired him for it.

Is Kalya climbing backwards up a path? A steep slope which is taking her some considerable time? Is she progressing, ever onwards, like a sleepwalker? Is she transforming the anguish of these last few days into a tragedy?

*

She has already turned round twice to seek out Sybil with her eyes. She will not turn round again. She trusts her, her grand-daughter will keep her word and stay under cover.

Three years ago, a little girl, dressed from head to toe in red wool, was running over a snowy field, among the silver birches... Kalya kept that photograph in her purse. Why had she not left the child back there, in a safe country, far from these dangers?

Nor will Kalya turn round to look at the fifth floor window, the one which earlier witnessed Myriam and Ammal's radiant progress. And then saw them still.

Now, elbows jostling, Odette and Slimane are leaning out of that same window. The pale face of the woman is very close to the dark face of the Sudanese.

Kalya moves forward. She does not attempt to imagine the outcome. She walks on, on. That is all.

*

No shadow moves in the square apart from her own. Perhaps the sniper is still lying in wait, hiding in a recess of a building? Armed by other hands? Or acting on his own impulse? Like a hunter infatuated with his gun, who when he feels like it will have a go at anything that moves?

Kalya moves forward towards the unknown. A happy ending: the two young women rise and hundreds of people throng towards them: Sybil, Odette and Slimane join in the general jubilation? Or will it be the other ending: the one which leads to the abyss?

The second alternative seems impossible. And yet, in the last few days, a shell fell on the square demolishing the Bazaar. The red shop – sandwiched between the buildings on either side – collapsed, killing Aziz the shopkeeper. He and Sybil had become friends.

Earlier, Kalya and Sybil had had to cut short their stay in the mountains on the advice of the hotel manager. It was more than a week since they had come back to stay with Odette until the airport, which had been closed as a precautionary measure, was reopened.

*

Kalya's thoughts contradict each other. The pounding of her heart grows louder.

From that mass of yellow cloth on which her gaze is firmly fixed, she sometimes hears the sound of a deathly groan and sometimes the breath of life...

EIGHT

Armadjian, the most reputable florist in town, has just delivered a gigantic bouquet.

'It's for you, Kalya. May I?'

Odette tears open the envelope:

'It's from Mario! I knew it was. He knew that you arrived yesterday. Five dozen roses! A gesture worthy of Farid. Such gentlemen, the men of this country! Have you ever come across that anywhere else?'

The flowers arrived a few hours before Mario's visit which Odette had carefully organized. Flitting from room to room, she gives orders to Slimane about the breakfast to be served on the verandah. She advises him to arrange the three wicker armchairs around the low table and to use the fine muslin tablecloth. Then she puts the flowers into half a dozen vases and knocks on her niece's door:

'You go and get dressed, Kalya! I'll see to the rest.'

Lowering her voice, she adds:

'He's a rich man. He's said to be worth... I can't remember how much, but it's a lot, ever such a lot of money.'

This habit the people here have of judging people by their bank accounts!

It is impossible to deprive Odette of her pleasures. She is going to transform a passing flirtation into a lasting romance, into an affair with a happy ending, and to organize a whole scenario around the two lead characters who have not seen each other for forty years. Convinced that in this day and age a child of twelve can be told everything, Odette has made Sybil her confidante.

'We must leave them alone. Don't come out of your room until I fetch you.'

*

Kalya darts a quick glance at the mirror. Steps back, then returns to her face which she is usually content to give but a passing glance in the morning.

Age has left its mark. Time's exhausting work has hardened her veins, withered her skin, softened the contours, made her eyelids droop and put shadows under her eyes. How should she react to such facts? Is not a life which so ill-treats one sometimes unacceptable? This life which comes to an untimely end or which moulders slowly away?

Life could be judged in that way but Kalya has a different perspective on it. Despite the years, she has preserved something of her youth. The thrills and impetuosity of youth slide gradually from the body to the soul and remain there alive.

A photographer, Kalya never wearies of that art, nor of a love which has weathered the seasons. She has known friendships, the richness of particular moments. Clouds have never blotted out the horizon for long. Life loves her and she loves it in return.

Odette's heavily powdered face peers round the half-open door: 'Are you ready? Your sweetheart will be here soon!'

VII

That evening, the music had enthralled me.

I had flown from my chair. Nothing could have stopped me! I could rely on Nouza's indulgence and the capriciousness of Farid whose whims often went beyond the bounds of respectability.

I danced, alone, amid the couples. Once they had recovered from their initial astonishment, they grew accustomed to my movements.

The rhythm of the music became slower. With his partner, whom he was holding closely, Mario crossed my path several times. The young woman was wearing a dull dress, beige with a white collar, and a high chignon perched on top of her head. She resisted and at the same time yielded to the insistent pressure of her partner. Her insipid face blushed as soon as he tried to rest his cheek against hers.

Mario was dressed less conventionally than the other young people: a bottle-green blazer over white flannel trousers, and a red and green striped tie. His raven black hair was wavy. His high cheekbones and his slightly drawn eyes made him look Asian. I no longer recall the shape of his nose. But I can picture his deep red lips. He had a sardonic expression.

He stopped in the middle of the dance, suddenly abandoned his partner and made his way towards me. He grabbed my wrist and held it forcefully in his hand. It radiated an electric heat.

'It's a pity you're so young, Kalya. A pity! But I'll find you again. I'll find you again, I promise.'

A smile, a look, music, words. Especially the words! A few words, a few seconds did the trick. I had fallen in love.

Nobody had noticed this brief interlude – except his partner with the chignon. Unless Odette had seen it too? She was gliding across the floor not far away on the arm of a sixty-year-old man whom Farid had picked out for her. The latter, too caught up by the memory of his flamboyant performances in Monte Carlo, refused to compromise himself in such a banal spin round the dance floor with his lifelong companion.

*

In the afternoons, my grandmother left me with Anaïs and shut herself in the gaming room. Everyone wanted to invite her to their table. Baccarat, bridge, poker, rummy – she slipped effortlessly from one card game to another. Nouza was quick with her hands, she had a good eye. She lost and won with the same cheerfulness.

Anaïs used to abandon me to go and join Henri, the shy, gangly young man. She would arrange to meet me two hours later at the foot of the lift.

I glimpsed them for the first time at the bottom of the hotel garden, coming out of a corrugated iron hut. They were glancing anxiously about them. Another time, going back up to my room before the arranged time, I found Anaïs's canvas shoes, her white cotton stockings and her orange floral printed dress in a heap in the doorway.

I turned round and tiptoed away before they saw me.

*

I only saw Mario on two other occasions. He often used to stroll down the main street of the village amid a crowd of boys and girls of whom he, at twenty-two, was the eldest. Sometimes the group would enter one of their homes from which the parents, who had gone into town, were temporarily absent. They smoked at leisure, drank in moderation and began love affairs which were limited to kisses and the light brushing of bodies. They called out to me to join them. Because of my youth, they soon tired of my company.

I left them to seek still further isolation in a corner of the Grand Hôtel garden. At one of the furthest tables – green, round, freshly painted – sitting on the very edge of the cane chair, I would amuse myself, wistfully, scraping the gravel with my shoes, in the wild hope of discovering a love letter among the stones. After a while, a waiter would bring me a glass of lemonade. As time went by, the fizzy drink would become increasingly flat and warm.

Then I saw Mario again. It was the eve of my departure.

Alone, he suddenly appeared on the steps and walked down with that assurance which never left him. He always wore crêpe-soled shoes which gave a spring to his step. He was coming straight towards me. He drew nearer. He was finally so close that he took the glass from my hands.

'You don't wear lipstick yet, so I'll have to guess where your lips touched the glass.'

He placed his own lips there and drank, slowly, his eyes half-closed, watching me through his eyelashes. My legs trembled. He returned the glass to me.

'I've left some. Your turn to drink now.'

He pointed to the light misty shadow that his mouth had left on the side of the glass.

'There. Place your mouth just there. And drink.'

I drank, gazing into his eyes. The sickly, warm mixture seemed to me the most magic of drinks.

Emerging from the revolving door of the hotel, Mario's group had just invaded the steps. The girls and boys made a splash of colour. Exuberant, in high spirits, they looked for Mario.

The girl with the chignon had let her hair down and it fell in shiny bronze waves over her shoulders. She had abandoned her dismal beige dress in favour of a red blouse and a brilliant white pleated skirt. She called out in confident, ringing tones:

'Mario! Are you coming?'

He turned round as he heard her call and waved to her. He had not had the slightest intention of lingering beside me and shouted:

'I'm coming right away!'

But again, before leaving, separating each syllable, he murmured in one breath:

'One day, I promise, I'll find you again.'

NINE

It was exactly nine o'clock. Mario rang the bell and stepped over the threshold of Odette's apartment. So many years had passed. 'I'll find you again' sounded ridiculous, pathetic. How would he reconcile the image of the little girl with the fiery gaze to that of a woman over fifty?

What troubled him even more was the scene his son had just made over Myriam. A law student, Georges was as brilliant a pupil as his father had been; the same self-assurance combined with a more intransigent, aggressive nature.

Georges did not approve of his sister's behaviour. In his opinion, she was involved in matters which did not concern women; she was becoming increasingly secretive and mysterious. The night before, she had not even come home.

Centuries of fathers, brothers and husbands, guardians of honour, had always surrounded mothers, sisters, wives and daughters. With Georges, these tendencies were innate, he did not even wish to discuss the matter. Under the pressure of new ideas, especially in the towns, customs were changing. But their roots, nourished by the same sap, held on, fitfully imposing behaviour that was as violent as it was outmoded.

Mario tried to calm his son.

'Myriam probably spent the night at Ammal's.'

'Is that all you have to say? Don't you think Ammal's family, who are practising Muslims, isn't just as shocked by such behaviour?'

'They are childhood friends.'

'They lead each other on.'

*

Left to the early morning rays shining through the royal blue
blind on the verandah, Kalya and Mario hardly dare look at
each other. Their present forms are projected on to their former
selves.

Odette bustles about, fills the coffee cups, butters the bread,
filling the air with her words. Dignified and silent, Slimane stays
in the background.

*

Odette ought to have told Kalya about Mario's marriage to a
deeply religious heiress, his countless female conquests and
recent death of his wife which had, surprisingly, thrown him
into disarray.

Angèle, his wife, had always made sure that he had no financial
or family worries. She was devoted enough to have her irascible
mother-in-law, Signora Laurentina, to stay with them in their
home until her death. An Italian who had emigrated to Lebanon
as a small child, she had married a young Lebanese. Throughout
her life, she had boasted of being 'from the north and of Milanese
origins', where an industrious and active population knew the
meaning of work.

'Not like those lazy southerners, from the heel of Italy, or the
people from these shores.'

She would often dart a disgruntled look in the direction of
her husband, a men's hairdresser who squandered his meagre
resources on backgammon, cards and the lottery.

Convinced that the keen air of her native Lombardy provided
a counterbalance to the mugginess of the Mediterranean shores
in Mario's blood, she was overjoyed at her son's success. His
brilliant studies had enabled him to climb the social ladder, to
leave behind his father's humble origins, and keep the company

only of those favoured by money and birth.

Since Angèle's death, Mario – convinced that only family ties could withstand hardship – had come up against the barrier that existed between Myriam and Georges. Until then, his wife had managed to hide it from him. The clashes that occurred in the country, in neighbouring regions, shook the two young people, intensifying their opposition to each other. It shattered their father.

Overnight, he gave up pursuing women, the ease with which he sailed from one affair to another or kept several going at the same time. He adopted an irreproachable code of conduct which would give him the authority, in future, so he thought, to preach high principles and family harmony.

*

Kalya looked as if she were 'passing through'. Passing through, like on that distant afternoon, in the garden of the Grand Hôtel, with her glass of lemonade in her hand.

Passing through, and at ease in that transitory state, as if she thought that existence itself were just that: a brief passage between two kinds of darkness. As if in the house of the flesh which was so perishable, or that of the spirit so changeable, or that of language in constant transformation, she recognized her only true habitats. Despite their precariousness, she felt more alive in them, less alienated, than in those stone dwellings, than in those places that were inherited, handed down, and which were often so deeply attached to the past and to their clods of earth that they forgot the space around them.

'Well, here we are!'

Suddenly dropping the roles that they had adopted over the years, Mario and Kalya have just uttered the same words and burst out in simultaneous laughter. Now they can gaze at each other in peace.

'What's the matter?'

Odette looks sulky. Those two are depriving her of an intrigue which she has carefully set up. They are thwarting her hopes of a romance which would have given her something to gossip about.

Forgetting her aunt's instructions, Sybil appears in her floral pyjamas, holding Julius.

The spell is broken all round. Resigned, Odette offers the child a stool and butters her a slice of bread.

'Do you want some date jam? It's a speciality.'

Sybil nods. She greets Mario by his first name and settles on her grandmother's lap.

'This is my son Sam's daughter.'

'I'd like to introduce you to my children. Especially Myriam...'

'Why "especially Myriam"?' Odette broke in. 'I thought it was Georges who gave you most pleasure!'

Kalya proceeds as if she has been walking for ever. From the beginning of time, she has been advancing step by step towards the heart of a great void. And yet she has only been walking for a few seconds, through an atmosphere laden with words and gasps. A walk that is immemorial and yet so short.

Inside her head, all is confusion. Is it Myriam or Ammal who is losing all that blood? Which of them is raising herself up, which of them is wounded? Will she manage to reach them? She does not know yet.

This square, this precisely defined space, is expanding, swelling, billowing with every ill wind. The relentless sound of gunfire, the pounding of hostile footsteps closes in on her. Then comes to die on the kerb. Not a word has been spoken yet. Anger might still die down. The day might still end well.

Words of death come to her lips. Suffering bodies from every age, from every corner of the earth, loom all around her. Short, unbroken waves, a procession of hope crashes against a concrete wall. Men long for death.

*

Kalya walks on without pausing, clutching at every glimmer of hope in her bid to escape anguish, to cover the final stretch. She must hurry. But at the same time, she ought not. The sniper might then panic and start shooting again.

She looks at the corner of a door, the corner of a window. Her gaze returns to that mound of yellow material, surrounded by the

70

reddish pool, towards these two young women whose thoughts and feelings she shares.

Kalya is no longer afraid, even if a cry hurtles through her from time to time, like a knife plunged into her stomach. She will reach the end. She will get there. There is so much strength in every human being. So much strength in her.

Shadows and light persist. Despair is grafted on to hope, hope on to despair.

*

Should she knock on a door and ask the occupants to come to their rescue? Behind the front line, in the nearby side streets, news spreads fast.

Odette moves away from the window and runs to the phone to call the police.

'Don't move, Slimane. Watch what happens. I'll be back.'

*

From the Blue Nile to the Green Nile, then from master to master, travelling from Upper to Lower Egypt, Slimane had begun his journey at the age of eight. His scarred cheeks bore the markings of his tribe. One fine day, fifty years ago, he had arrived on Farid's doorstep and had never left him. Depending on his mood, the latter sometimes called him 'my son', and sometimes 'stupid ass'.

They had grown old together, day by day, sharing the ups and downs of a long life, emigrating one last time from Cairo to Beirut. Slimane would gaze towards the horizon where places melt into one another to meet on a calm, unchanging line. His black skin has the sheen of pebbles and his eyes the coolness of the shade. Since Farid's death, Odette and her possessions are his entire world. Nothing grates within him.

Everything slides into his indulgent heart with a brushing of wings.

Slimane looks out of the window. His heartbeat remains steady, but a vague disquiet clings to him like a cloud.

He recognizes Kalya. His gaze, misty with old age, is unable to distinguish the two young women in the coloured heap in the middle of the square. He wonders where the child is. Even if he leans out, he cannot see her in the doorway.

*

Kalya grips the pistol. This gun, which she refused three days earlier when Georges insisted she keep it, and which he had left in the chest of drawers in the hall, despite her protests. Then suddenly, she had not hesitated to grab it. Now, she is aiming it in front of her. Will she use it? Will she know how to use it?

She looks constantly about her, trying to see, to foresee. Aiming at the dark, masked hatred, which has come from who knows where, she advances. Ammal and Myriam must live. She wants to live too. Sybil's face flashes into her mind and smiles at her. She has never experienced anything brighter, more alive, than that face. She delights in the memory of it.

*

The sight of this square, ripped to shreds, of this city spewing weapons of death from its entrails, the sight of men, women and children caught in the lethal cloudburst and senseless hail of bullets is not even possible to imagine. Not yet.

Kalya's heart is racing, like that of this town tormented then abandoned by anguish. The woman sets out, as in a dream, along this path which stretches away before her...

TEN

The doorbell rang. Slimane made his way into the hall. Picking up her tortoise, Sybil rushed past, reached the door ahead of him and opened it.

Surprised, the young woman thought she was on the wrong floor. She was wearing jeans and a pink blouse. Her black bushy hair shaded a lively face with fine features.

The child kissed her on both cheeks and introduced herself:

'My name's Sybil. I arrived yesterday with my grandmother Kalya.'

'Is my father...?'

'You mean Mario?'

'Yes.'

The little girl shouted in the direction of the verandah:

'It's Myriam!'

'You know my name?'

The child relieved her of her soft, red shoulder bag and pushed Myriam ahead of her playfully. The latter frowned slightly – by now, an expression of seriousness was set in her face. The sun was not at its strongest. The morning was still mild and gentle. The wicker chairs, the laid table, Slimane's discreet and thoughtful presence, this newcomer's pleasant face and Odette's enthusiastic welcome made her want to be lighthearted, to forget the grimness of the outside world. She leaned over her father, and put her arms around him.

'Georges told me you were worried. I came to reassure you. In this country, Kalya, even when you're grown up, you're still accountable to your family, to your father and brother. Especially to your brother!'

73

She managed to laugh about it, and ruffled Mario's hair.

'Oh yes we are, don't protest. Go ahead and ask your questions.'

'Were you at Ammal's place?'

'Where else would I be?'

'The exams are finished, what have you still got to talk about?'

'Oh, lots of things.'

'Are you cooking something up, or what?' he retorted jokingly and immediately tried to make amends.

'At your age, you can dream...'

Then he held out his hands:

'Stay with us for a while.'

*

She stayed. Bluish rays filtered through the blind, tingeing their faces and trailing across the floor and walls. She crouched on the floor and resumed her grave expression. Giving Kalya a sidelong glance, she wondered about this woman whose arrival Mario had been awaiting.

She was a fairly well-known photographer, he had told her. Was it true? What sort of photos was she interested in?

'Are you here on holiday or for work?'

'On holiday. Purely on holiday. My time is all Sybil's.'

To Myriam, that word 'holiday', repeated several times, seemed strange, almost embarrassing.

'Why come here for a holiday?'

'I've been thinking about it for a long time, so has Sybil.'

'I'm the one who wanted to come. It was my idea, wasn't it, Kalya?'

Myriam continued to stare at this woman. She seemed to her both remote and accessible at the same time. Her attentive gaze wandered occasionally, as if she were trying to absorb the foreign climate.

Kalya was probably far from imagining what was in the offing. She was oblivious, but in a completely different way from Odette and her entourage. For they hung onto boats that let in water everywhere, obstinately clinging to the sails of memory.

'I would like you to tell me your impressions before you leave.'

A panoramic bay, sumptuous hotels, private beaches, gleaming cars, archaeological sites, luxury and leisure, the combined pleasures of the East and the West: that was how the country appeared! An absolute dream. Were those the images that Kalya would take back with her? Picturesque postcards, sun-drenched slides, blissful sights?

Myriam would have liked to start up a conversation and say to her: 'Not that! Don't take that back! There's more, there's better and there's worse.' A blend of faces, customs, beliefs, fertile land and arid soil. New slopes and ancient shores. Two halves of the same creature: one profile modern, the other archaic. Complex, overlapping worlds, the opposite of Odette's shimmering universe. Their little land was seriously ill, but nobody would admit it. Still sparkling under the balm of prosperity, it concealed its fevers, its crises, its torpor. The contrasts were part of the magic. Foreigners and tourists considered it both generous and grasping, loved its joie de vivre, took offence at its display of wealth, went into raptures over its warmheartedness and welcome and made fun of its bragging. They admired its cultures, rebuked it for its inordinate taste for money, were amazed at its strange mixture of sectarianism and freedom, of affability and sudden fury. A small country that had become the centre of intense arms trafficking, dealers from all four corners of the earth furthering their careers on the spot. Here, everything could be negotiated. Weapons recovered from neighbouring battlefields, revolvers from a brief civil war replaced by more modern devices, sophisticated weaponry requiring the presence of technicians and instructors.

Could she explain such things to Kalya, so that she would not leave as lightly as she had come? So that she would not take back false impressions and false photos?

One had to be locked away from society, like Odette and many others, to see nothing, to have no sense of foreboding. But Myriam held her tongue as she had become accustomed to doing. It was neither the time nor the place to talk to Kalya, though her eyes, at times, did seem to be questioning her.

Sitting beside the little girl, who was lovingly patting the tortoise's wrinkled head, Myriam stroked her shining hair. Smooth, flowing hair which stirred with every movement, a fiery blonde, as seen only in the cinema. So different from her own which was thick and dark, drawn back in a tight weft. What was there in common between her world and Sybil's? They were both privileged, but in such different ways. Modernism and simplicity in Sybil. A more fragmented modernism in Myriam, a flashier type of affluence.

In the child's universe, essential problems were either resolved or dismissed. Here, they burst on the surface, became more and more pressing, more and more acute.

VIII

Framed by white wood beading, the little photo of my grandfather Nicolas, placed at the foot of the icon, could have passed unnoticed. Its smallness, the modest choice of frame did not conform at all to Nouza's tastes; and yet she had chosen them to satisfy her late husband's wish for simplicity.

My grandfather died of pneumonia when I was seven. I loved and admired him for many reasons.

His bedroom, separate from the rest of the huge household, was at the end of a dark corridor. It was adjacent to the staircase which led down to the kitchens.

My grandfather loved his food. Several times a day, he would go down the few stairs which took him to Constantin. The cook was always delighted to see him. He offered him the first taste of an hors d'oeuvre or a dessert, or one of those round, flat, warm loaves which he stuffed with black olives and goat's cheese, and onto which he poured a trickle of oil and sprinkled the occasional mint leaf. Nicolas preferred these little pleasures to regular meals. Despite this, his appearance never changed and he remained until the very end of medium build, his stomach hardly rounded. He preferred to skip lunch or dinner rather than forfeit these forays – both friendly and gastronomic – into the kitchen. He had a good time there, sitting at the same table as Constantin whose company he enjoyed much more than that of Nouza's guests.

*

Once, he invited me into his bedroom. I can picture him now, leaning against the wide open door:

77

'Come in, little Kalya.'

I entered an area of brilliant whiteness, so different from cousin Mitry's gloomy lair. The curtains were of natural linen, the walls whitewashed and the camp bed was covered with waffle cloth. The table, chair and wardrobe were lacquered white. A lot of empty space.

My grandfather's appearance was bright and sunny, too: a greying moustache, silver hair frizzing at the temples and eyes of a transparent blue. He always wore the same brown trousers which had been bleached in the wash, and a chalk-white, open-necked shirt.

The child of an immigrant, Nicolas together with a few others had introduced silk worm farming to Egypt, his adoptive land. Gifted in finance and business – even though without formal education – my grandfather thought it was his duty to put his talents to making a profit. 'Getting rich' remained for him an intellectual game, an exercise in intelligence and determination. Effort and performance appealed to him. And yet he rejected the material results for his own benefit. He felt awkward the minute he found himself in opulent surroundings, like Nouza's. So as not to hinder her, he had chosen to live in seclusion.

Moving from one business to the next, Nicolas had made a fortune. He soon found himself owning three buildings in the city and several hectares of agricultural land which he rented out to peasants.

Despite this prosperity, my grandfather still had the tastes of a poor man. What he most enjoyed was the company of the most deprived people. Money and success remained abstract notions which only took on a concrete form through the comfort he was able to bestow on his loved ones.

His generosity extended itself even to the penniless members of his family. Foutine, Nouza'a mother, whose civil servant husband had died ruined, and cousin Mitry were permanent members of the household. Not to mention the countless relatives who never went away empty-handed. Nicolas kept a secret kitty, into which he often delved, for other misfortunes, in which the country abounded.

As for Nouza, his wife, several years his junior, her beauty which both dazzled and intimidated him, deserved in his opinion the best possible setting. He took pleasure in offering her a house, garden, numerous servants, a car and chauffeur, jewelry and clothes. He let her travel as she pleased but rarely joined her.

Nicolas subscribed annually to a box at the Opera House for her, while he was content to listen to the great arias from *Aida*, *Tosca*, and *Manon Lescaut* on his wind-up gramophone. He kept two seats at the racecourse, happy that she was able to go there, elegant, dressed up and more often than not accompanied by her brother Farid, who, like his sister, loved society life.

*

When his grandchildren came to visit, my grandfather 'went upstairs to the parlour'. After the meal, he would go down on all fours in front of the red velvet settee, invite the boys to climb on to his back and carry them from room to room pretending he had to surmount various obstacles. The children often lost their balance and fell on the floor. My grandfather taught them to hold back their tears, to transform each fall into a cheerful joke. Convinced that the girls – a more tearful race – would not be able to react so healthily, he never offered them a ride.

One day, I caught him off-guard. I jumped on to his back and clung to his shoulders:

'Forward, Grandpa!'

He was unable to resist. I earned myself a long, bumpy ride. To show him what I was made of, I deliberately fell to the tiled floor.

The shock was more violent than I had anticipated. Nouza

fussed and came rushing to pick me up. My grimaces turned into a smile, into a peal of laughter. I was on my feet. My grandfather was holding his hand out to me.

'You deserve to have been called Kalil! Not Kalya.'

Fortified by this supreme compliment, I dashed to the bathroom to splash water on my painful forehead and my scratched knees.

From then on, he was assiduous in his attentions to me, and even invited me into his room on several occasions.

*

He died too soon. Before the questions I would have liked to ask him had formed. Questions which were probably his, but which he did not want to impose on Nouza, for fear of marring a carefree and, when all is said and done, harmonious existence.

*

On All Soul's Day, Nouza sometimes took me to my grandfather's tomb. The cemetery, along with others belonging to the many Christian communities, was in a suburb of Cairo, close to the densely populated parts of the city.

Carrying a large wreath of red gladioli, Nouza walked among the tombs, along the avenue of eucalyptus trees, stopping under the leafy branches to breathe in their fragrance.

'Do as I do, Kalya, it clears the lungs.'

I tottered after her, clutching a large pot of russet chrysanthemums. The large, compact flowers partly blocked my view.

Omar, the chauffeur, followed us carrying an armful of lilies, which symbolized for my grandmother the integrity of the deceased.

As a Muslim, he was not indifferent to these rituals; he had never known my grandfather, but he respected the dead. Like some of his fellow Muslims, he had a strong affection for the saint of Lisieux, that little Thérse, laden with roses, whose church was a few miles from the capital. On one occasion when his mother had just been cured, Omar even added a commemorative plaque to the hundreds of others at the foot of her statue.

In front of the family mausoleum, Nouza hastily untied the ribbons, tore open the wrapping and strewed the tiled floor with scarlet and lily-white flowers. I placed the pot of rigid chrysan-themums to one side. The sun was at its peak, in a few hours time these plants would wilt. What did it matter! What counted was the gesture, the spread and even the waste. It made the tribute paid even more precious.

Elias, the cemetery keeper, appeared surrounded by a laughing, ragged horde of children, with his wife who was pregnant for the eleventh time. With heavy eyelids, dragging behind him his watering hose which leaked in several places, he was making his way towards Nouza.

Immediately he forestalled her. The cleaning of the vault had been neglected, he knew. He reeled off the causes: deaths and illnesses, desert winds, chasing after thieves. Then he swore he would sweep up, get rid of all the dust with great jets of water:

'Come back in three days, in two days. Come back tomorrow! You'll see.'

The gilt epitaphs will shine, the mottling of the marble and the stone festoons and garlands will reappear. Promise, I swear it! He would like his children to be witness but they had already scattered among the tombs and were playing with a half-threadbare rubber ball. He called them back, waving his arms. They knew his story by heart and replied, echoing one another, with shrieks and laughter:

'I promise, I swear it! I swear it, I promise!'

Her hands resting on her stomach, her eyes drooping, his wife nodded, sighing.

After Nouza's departure – she would not be back for another

long year – Elias would sink back into his indolence and forget his promises.

Pretending to believe his oaths, my grandmother distributed notes and coins to the children who suddenly came running from all four corners of the cemetery. They skipped and hopped around her, their hands outstretched. Their eyes and the corners of their mouths were sticky with flies, and glimpses of thigh, stomach and shoulders could be seen through their ragged clothes.

'Take my purse, Kalya. Give them everything that's in it.'

Her lightheartedness shocks me. I am ashamed, I look elsewhere, I walk away.

'I can't.'

My white cotton socks are too neat, my red patent leather shoes with buckles shine under the film of dust.

A little girl of my age runs after me. She has just grabbed the hem of my blue silk skirt and is holding me back. With an ecstatic look, she rubs the silky material between her thumb and index finger. I watch her, transfixed. I wish the earth would swallow me up, or that we could exchange dresses, or that I could kiss her and take her home with us.

'My name's Salma, what's yours?'

Her huge eyes look right through me. She smiles with curiosity and concern.

'What's yours?'

ELEVEN

The previous night had been harsh. Ammal and Myriam had just learned that armed men had held up a bus in the middle of the city and murdered ten passengers. The same day, in the surrounding countryside, others had discovered at the foot of an embankment the mutilated corpses of five young people.

Who had started it? Which act had come first? The threads were already becoming tangled. Already hatred was beginning to match the thirst for revenge.

*

Sitting in the drawing room, Georges tapped his foot on the floor, switched the radio on and off and smoked cigarette after cigarette, waiting for Myriam to return. As soon as she appeared, he rose and barred her path.

'What time do you call this?'

Instead of replying, she asked where her father was.

'You've forgotten, he's at Odette's. He went on enough about his "amorous encounter". Another of his old flames! What about you, where have you been?'

The girl shrugged and went off to her room. He joined her, then, catching the strap of her red shoulder bag, he seized her arm and spun her round forcefully to face him:

'Will you answer me?'

Myriam managed to escape him again.

'I have nothing to tell you.'

She ran to the door of the apartment and slammed it behind her. This time, he did not try to follow her.

She leaned against the wall for a few minutes to get her breath back. Then she rang Odette's doorbell.

*

Georges was resentful towards his father for many things: for his weakness towards Myriam, and for what he had made Angèle endure. A wife above reproach, an exemplary mother! And yet, she had never held him. Later, she had never kissed him, except on rare occasions on the forehead. Had Georges suffered as a result? He did not want to think about it.

Disappointed and humiliated by Mario, Angèle was wary of any other contact. Her son only wanted to remember her as a pious, respectable woman who never sought to push herself forward or to hold her family up to ridicule.

Another image haunted him. He could picture his mother seated with her hands crossed. In the evenings, she would sit very close to the lamp with the mauve lampshade which stood on the pedestal table. Mario was never there, Angèle seemed to be forever waiting for him, starting at the slightest sound on the landing. In the subdued light, her cheeks were tinged with purple streaks. Her thin hair, cut in urchin style with a black fringe, did nothing to soften her features. Her brown eyes flecked with gold had the look of a doe at bay. On such occasions, Georges felt ready to fight for her, to defend her against the father who had made her suffer.

At every opportunity, Angèle would take a rosary out of her pocket and pray. She prayed for Georges, for Myriam and for the unfaithful Mario, for their nearest and dearest, for neighbours and relatives scattered all over the world. She even prayed for her mother-in-law, Laurentina, no doubt purging her irascible temper in Purgatory. She also prayed for her small homeland, pitying from the depths of her heart those whom life's lottery had caused to be born outside the Catholic religion. Then she extended her prayers to the whole world, placing her hopes in the conversion of the planet which would resolve all the problems, all the infidelities and all the wars and which should come about, according to the Scriptures, before the end of time.

After the death of his wife, Mario began attending Church. As if the departure of that precious intercessor between him and the heavens – who, with her novenas and indulgence, had absolved him of his sins – left him defenceless and with no guarantees in the face of a relentless future.

Unlike Georges, Myriam was outraged by her mother's narrow existence. She had suffered from the lack of physical contact and did not hide the fact. Antagonistic from childhood to this frigid, pious temperament, she swore she would be completely different. And she was, by nature.

She would choose the man of her life and they would love each other passionately. She would shower her children with kisses.

She would never allow Georges to impede her desires, to thwart her plans or to change her outlook. Or Mario either. But he was more subtle, easier to handle. He allowed himself to be influenced by each of his children in turn.

*

From the moment they burst out laughing at the same time, Mario abandoned, with relief, his swaggering air. With Kalya, he suddenly felt at ease, rid of that cocksure, ambitious image that he had created for himself and which was becoming an increasing burden.

He decided not to question Myriam about her absence. She was chatting to Sybil who was asking her endless questions. She had none of the shyness, none of the awkwardness of little girls of long ago. Kalya admired that ease, that open face, those bubbling words. She was moved too by her curiosity; turned towards Myriam, the child wanted to know about everything.

Julius was peacefully munching his lettuce leaf. Under the verandah blind, the bluish shade was changing to white, heralding the hottest part of the morning.

'Let's go into the living room, we'll be cooler there,' said Odette.

Slimane had already closed the shutters.

*

'Do you remember, Kalya, our houses in Egypt? Oases from the scorching heat and dust outside.'

Entering the dimmed room, Kalya was once again able to relax her muscles and rest her eyes from the burning light. Once again, she felt pleasure as her skin absorbed the half-darkness, the pleasure of a view immersed in a liquid tranquillity which softens corners and outlines.

Beads of sweat formed on Sybil's forehead, at the roots of her hair where the blonde was even blonder. The heat did not affect the little girl who adapted to everyone and everything. With quiet composure, her eyes alert, she spoke to one person then another, then returned to Myriam, questioning her about this country and its inhabitants, about herself, her age and her future career. Finally, standing in front of Myriam, her hands on her waist, she said:

'I'm going to be a dancer!'

'A dancer!'

Imagining the effect of this declaration on Farid, Odette jumped. She could hear him saying: 'My great niece on stage? Never! All that, it's the Folies Bergères and the like!' Confused, she turned to Kalya.

'Did you hear? "A dancer!"'

A dancer! Kalya smiled at the child, at that procession of women going back in time. Smiled at the grandmother playing her zither inlaid with mother-of-pearl, accompanying her daughter's swaying; at Foutine, the great-grandmother, undulating on the black and white tiles of the Governor's house, a chiffon handkerchief at her fingertips. At Nouza, moving gracefully in the arms of a partner; at herself under the pergola, capering about on the banqueting table. Smiled at all those dances.

Sybil gave the tortoise to Myriam to hold and performed on the spot. A pirouette, an entrechat, a jeté. The pale sheet of hair fanned out around her. She finished with a cabriole, followed by the splits.

'You will be a dancer!'

Myriam clapped with all her strength. She envied this child from across the seas. In her country, she would not encounter any obstacles to her talents. She often wished she could go away, live elsewhere, have only her own future to build. Here, you had to take into account families, customs, religions and backgrounds. You were trapped, caught in a stranglehold. How could you escape it? Above all, how could you remain indifferent to the upheavals, the creakings that were gradually undermining the whole region? How could you not be concerned and worried about them, not seek to bring about changes while it was still possible? The recent troubles were likely to have severe repercussions. Should she warn Kalya? Advise her to leave as soon as possible with the child? Or, in the hope that they were just violent accidents that would soon pass, should she, on the contrary, give them time? They seemed so happy to get to know each other here. Especially in this land here.

Together with Ammal and their increasing number of friends, they had to decide on a plan of action which would halt the spiral.

'Kalya, I'll introduce you to Ammal.'

Myriam felt she could trust the stranger. She would have liked to talk to her, to confide her disarray and convictions. It was neither the place nor the time. The opportunity would arise later. The previous night, the young woman had not had a wink of sleep, that too added to the confusion.

*

Odette had just slipped a chain with a blue stone and a medallion on it around Sybil's neck:

'The blue is to ward off the evil eye.'

'What's the evil eye?'

Odette crinkled her forehead and launched into a confused anecdotal explanation.

'The medallion will protect you too. I had it blessed in Lourdes. Look, it's the Immaculate Conception, do you recognize it?'

'The Immaculate what?'

'Sam was never religious,' said Kalya apologetically.

'He had his daughter baptized, at least? Have you been baptized, Sybil?'

'Baptized? I think so.'

'What about Jesus? You know who Jesus and Saint Joseph and the Holy Virgin are? Have you heard of the Holy Virgin?'

'Do you mean Mama Mary?'

'Mama Mary?'

'I love Jesus very much. I know all about him. I love him and Mama Mary very much.'

Kalya smiled. Nouza's icon, now berated, now worshipped, emerged from the recesses of her memory.

Frowning, Odette added with a note of reproach:

'Mama Mary, is that what you call the Mother of God?'

*

'What's your name?'

'Ammal. What's yours?'

'Myriam.'

Perched on a hill, the school commands on all sides a view of the sea. The playground stretches towards slopes bordered with olive trees and pines. The two little girls are hurtling down them in pursuit of a ball. It bounces faster and faster over the stones.

'Here, you can have it.'

'Keep it, it's yours.'

Up above, their friends call to them to come back and finish the game. They clamber back up hand in hand. Ammal wears plaits with blue ribbons, Myriam has a dark mop with tight curls, held in place with red slides. They run, drawing apart and back together again, and pull each other up the slope, dancing around the tree trunks. They pant, laugh and stop to catch their breath and look at the sea.

'Do you often go to the seaside?'

'Sometimes.'

'I can swim. Can you?'

'Not yet.'

'One day, I'll go away.'

'Where?'

'Over there.'

One after the other, they point to the horizon.

They are seven, eight, ten, twelve years old. They ask themselves and each other questions; those burning, serious childhood questions.

'Does your God have a different name from mine?'

'He's called Allah, but it's the same.'

'Do you think it's the same?'

'It's the same.'

'I think so too.'

'We pray to him differently, that's all.'

They are twelve, thirteen, sixteen. They borrow each other's exercise books, textbooks, combs and mirrors; they exchange dresses and pullovers.

They are seventeen, eighteen. They reject certain customs, certain habits. Sometimes a snap of the fingers is enough for the boundaries to disappear; at other times, they are like tenacious old oak trees whose roots will always grow again. The days add up, weeks and months fly by.

They are nineteen. They leave the wealthy district. They want to see, to know. They enter those suburbs built alongside the towns, those villages dotted about in the arid mountains. They speak to those children who wade about in puddles of mud, to those emaciated or bloated women abandoned by life, to those feverish youngsters deprived of a future. They come and go, trying to understand the meaning of life, the significance of all this. They devour books and newspapers and make friends.

They are twenty. They rearrange their questions, stepping over routines and prejudices in one stride; make a pact against everything that separates and divides.

'There will never be a split between us.'

'Never.'

'You won't change, whatever happens?'

'Whatever happens!'

One studies to be a lawyer, the other to be a pharmacist. Their families wish to see them married, settled, endowed with children, abandoning studies which they hope are temporary.

Different from their mothers, they are slim, with tiny breasts, long legs and a relaxed appearance. They speak openly of love. They experience it passionately and with difficulty, caught between freedom and taboos. Boys are simultaneously fascinated and perturbed by them.

They confide little in these mothers who are too passive or too fidgety, frittering away their idle lives half asleep or in social chit-chat. Ammal sometimes visits her silent, veiled grandmother. It is as though age had freed her tongue. Gentle and smiling, she has watched half a century slip by, watched the breaking down of an old world and the fermentation of a new one which has not yet matured. She encourages her grand-daughter:

'Learn as much as you can. Live. I didn't know anything. I don't even know if I've lived. Learn too, both of you, to know each other.'

They clash with their fathers and brothers. Face up to gossip. The universe comes to them in waves and echoes. They are living through changing, fertile times. Vigilant, they maintain openness between one group and another. There are many who desire it. And yet they know that those who think differently are numerous too.

*

'All that I tell you about when we were growing up will seem so different to you, Kalya.' She added with a hint of irritation:

'So far removed from your Paris!'

IX

Paris! Can one love a city like a person? And yet that is how I loved it.

My grandmother had just left the gaming room. As soon as she saw me, she came towards me, her face radiant, a smile on her lips. You could never tell from her expression whether she had lost or won. In the garden of the Grand Hôtel, she led me to her favourite table, the one by the oleander hedge.

'I miss Paris! Do you remember, Kalya, four years ago we were there together. You were only eight, you can probably barely remember it.'

And yet I did remember it. The mere name, 'Paris', made me feel liberated, body and soul swept up in exhilaration.

'Always the same old faces, always the same words, the same games! I'm bored, I'm stifled here.'

My grandmother added that, since Nicolas's death, she could no longer afford such a long and costly trip.

'Five days on a liner, trains and hotels. But I'll return there before I die.'

'You won't die, Grandma. You're still young.'

She pinched my cheek.

'You can talk!'

Nouza took a tortoiseshell powder compact out of her bag, opened it and scrutinized the mirror. Her fifty-six years had left their mark on her complexion and on the contours of her face. She slapped her hand on her neck, stretched the skin which had sagged and glanced at the mirror again.

'No, no, it would be pointless!'

She shook her head and clicked her tongue several times

92

against the roof of her mouth in mockery at this useless gesture. Offering me her smile and her lively blue gaze, she straightened up, moved her shoulders and shook her legs, testing her back muscles and the strength of her calves.

'I'll still pass muster. But I want to see Paris again before I'm too old.'

Nouza would not grow 'too old'.

*

Five years later, at the door of her Cairo home – amidst a wardrobe-trunk, a clutter of suitcases and a hat-box which Omar the chauffeur had begun to place in the boot of the car – my grandmother collapsed. Cut down like a beautiful tree.

I was told that she had been holding her passport, her ticket marked 'Marseilles' and that they had a hard job getting her to let go of them.

I was far away. In Paris, at boarding school. The summer of the Grand Hôtel was the last one we spent together.

*

Nouza stretched out her arm behind her, broke off an oleander branch, stuck three pink flowers in her blouse and offered the others to me.

'Is it true, Kalya, you remember Paris?'

It was August. She had rented an apartment in Auteuil, at the bottom of a cul-de-sac called 'Jouvence'. In order to come and go as she pleased, she engaged a governess who took me out for walks. She was a Swiss woman, with an ample bosom and small grey eyes who was exasperated by the big city.

I fell in love with this city at first sight.

'Paris, queen of the world!' my great-uncle Farid would croon each time he returned.

In Cairo, I scarcely knew the streets, and public transport was a forbidden sphere. I came and went within a closed world of private houses. All around, further away, moved other worlds whose existence I was totally unaware of, and which I would probably never encounter. And yet, the call of those worlds tormented me.

After leaving the house, I dragged my governess, despite her reluctance, into the metro. I rushed down with delight, savouring that particular smell which comes from the damp stone, underground, and from the people crowded together.

Running ahead of my chaperone, I galloped down the stairs and threaded my way through the crowd. Inside the compartment, I stared at those countless, passing, anonymous faces. I made up a story about each one. I loved watching the stations go past; I learned all their names by heart. I recognized the ads: Dubo Dubon Dubonnet, Cadum Baby Powder, Wonder batteries, Meunier chocolate, Eclipse shoe polish.

Leaning against the rail of the platform at the rear of the bus, I would let the sun and rain beat down on my face. I drank in with my eyes every corner of the city. During our walks along the banks of the Seine or along the avenues lined with glittering shop windows, the Swiss woman would sigh for her lakes, her mountain paths and her sort of trees which 'grew out of the earth, not the tarmac'. She complained of the din, of the filthy air. Her negativity dampened my enthusiasm, but I soon bounced up again, letting my wings, my breath all carry me away.

The governess led me across the Tuileries gardens, allowed me a few goes on the swings and helped me climb onto a wooden roundabout. She never congratulated me on catching those rings which I jangled around my stick. She snatched out of my hands the red and yellow striped lollipop I had just won and threw it to the bottom of a litter bin.

'It's full of germs! I'll never allow you to eat that!'

To console me, she would buy me a hoop or a skipping rope, which I mislaid in no time.

*

Beside the large pond, I could no longer hold myself back. I took advantage of a moment of inattention to escape, alone, towards the Rue de Rivoli. The governess ran after me, but I had no difficulty in giving her the slip.

Free! I was free! I allowed myself to go where my footsteps took me.

I crossed the courtyard of the Louvre, mingling with the passers-by, found myself facing the embankment, went up the Rue de l'Arbre Sec, the Rue Vauvilliers and the Rue du Jour! Their names are still music in my ears. I ended up on the Quai de la Mégisserie. Picking my way between the cars and a tourist coach, I crossed over and continued as far as the Pont des Arts.

Stopping for breath, I leaned on the parapet and gazed and thought. Images of water, of the sky, the flowing river, clouds, barges gliding beneath the arches: I travelled. The permanence of the buildings, their domes, their columns and their history: I put down roots there. I was enraptured. It was so beautiful I could have cried!

Later, accompanied by droplets of rain, I found my way back to the apartment without getting lost.

*

I went in, my cheeks hot, flushed, with enthusiasm and spirit, just as the tearful governess was offering her resignation.

I was surprised, scared by my grandmother's pallor. I realized what a fright I had given her.

'It's so beautiful, Grandma. So beautiful!'

That was all I could think to say. It was enough, for Nouza took me in her arms and decided not to scold me.

I was bursting with affection for her, for Paris and for the whole world. I ran over to my Swiss governess, flung my arms around her neck and apologized, swearing I would never do it again.

She withdrew her resignation.

But a few days later, she was summoned home urgently to be with her brother who had just undergone an operation: she was not sorry to leave us. Nouza suspected false pretences. She shrugged her shoulders and took me by the hand:

'Governesses aren't for us, Kalya. Nor are we for them! We'll manage on our own, just the two of us.'

*

For a week, there was just Nouza and me. In the evening, when my grandmother went out – she had friends, acquaintances, her company was much sought – our neighbour would pop in from time to time to make sure that I was all right.

The theatre programmes piled up on a velvet pouffe. Through photographs, I become acquainted with Josephine Baker, Mistinguett, Maurice Chevalier, Georges Milton, Damia, Yvonne Printemps, Lucienne Boyer, Pils and Tabet...

There were never any newspapers lying around the apartment. Nouza hardly bothered about what was happening in the world. Nicolas had tried in vain to get her to take an interest.

It was 1928. The Paris Pact which made America a European ally, had just been signed. Mussolini was hammering out his hostile declarations, his chin jutting out further and further. Organizing in the wings, Hitler was emerging from the shadow of Hindenburg. Briand was trying to outlaw war. An economic crisis was about to engulf the world.

*

Two or three times I overheard Nouza on the telephone. She carelessly left the doors between us open. Her voice took on a strange and pathetic note.

One evening, it was heartbreaking. Her words were faltering, repetitive and interspersed with sighs. I restrained myself from rushing to her aid. I heard:

'So, it's over? It's over.'

I did not dare understand.

She finally emerged from her room, her face much paler than it was on the day I had run away.

*

We took a carriage to the ship which was to take us back to Alexandria. A taxi drove in front of us carrying Nouza's countless suitcases.

The day before, Farid had telephoned from Montecatini, announcing that he would be voyaging on the *Champollion* with us.

As soon as she was hidden under the leather hood, Nouza dissolved into tears. I can visualize the scene with limpid clarity. My grandmother was wearing a jade green dress, matching shoes and a turquoise hat with a veil which she raised from time to time to dab at her eyes with a handkerchief of the same colour. The inside of the carriage reminded me of a brownish grotto.

'Why are you crying, Grandma?'

'Paris! I'll never see Paris again.'

It was my turn to burst into tears.

'I love Paris too!'

She put her arms round my shoulders and hugged me to her. I felt as though our breath was being snatched away from us, our freedom; and that we would never return together to the lost city.

The *Champollion* was alongside the quay. Hand in hand and red-eyed, we climbed up the gangway that led to the big white ship. My great-uncle was nowhere to be seen. Soon, they would be weighing anchor.

Suddenly, leaning over the rail, we saw him. He was running up and down the landing stage trying to catch a glimpse of us. We waved to him. He shouted in our direction, getting his words mixed up, explaining that he had been delayed by urgent business and would join us in a couple of weeks. Nouza concluded that despite his telephone call the previous day, he had met somebody and that he had fallen in love again.

Seeking forgiveness, Farid produced a pile of presents which filled his arms.

'For you, my darling sister. And for the little one!', He had combed the shops, spent without counting the cost! For him, 'spending' was the most intoxicating pleasure; 'thrift' the most loathsome thing in the world.

The gangway had just been raised. Farid desperately sought a way to get the presents to us.

He saw a young seaman who was entering the hold of the liner, and entrusted them to him with a fat tip.

The sailor gave us the parcels out at sea as Marseilles faded on the horizon.

In the square, everything is quiet, behind the walls the voices have fallen silent. Kalya advances alone.

Her vacation in the mountains with Sybil had been abruptly curtailed. Then, since their second stay at Odette's, other troubles had erupted, other clashes had taken place. Certain sectors of the town had been plunged into darkness for a few hours. There were rumours of arms confiscation, the wailing sirens of ambulances had been heard.

This path from the porch, where the little girl is still standing, to the heap of yellow cloth spattered with blood, is beset with memories, vacillating, stretching time, mingling with dreadful images: columns of prisoners, fields of corpses, painful cities, London under the blitzkrieg, Paris occupied. Will the world never stop enduring these tortures? This city here, still shining over the sea, will it in turn sink into the abyss?

Where does this path lead? Kalya does not know. Time can no longer be measured. Sometimes it can be compressed in one's hand, at others it dissipates and blows away in the wind.

Will the woman suddenly stop still? Her lips tremble, her skin tingles. A shaft of fire pierces her heart.

Life holds on, however, takes a new breath and is rekindled.

Her legs move forwards, leading, following: one step after another, a step, then a step, and a step. Then a step...

At times, Kalya becomes aware of her body again; of the soles of her feet rubbing against the soles of her sandals, of the repetitive movement of her thighs, of her skirt swirling around her calves, of the tension in her neck. She recognizes and feels the hard, rough butt of the revolver.

Around her, nothing seems to be breathing. Even the birds and their beating wings have gone.

*

Kalya moves on in a nightmare. A danger threatens, invisible ties fetter her knees, she cannot progress, she sinks to her ankles in the mire. She could be, she would like to be, elsewhere. In another country, another world, on another path. Is death awaiting her at the end of this one?

Nicolas had gone with a smile, stretched out on his narrow camp bed. The sun, at its zenith, brought to his bare room all its brilliant whiteness. Holding her ticket, Nouza had collapsed amid a clutter of trunks, suitcases and boxes. Anaïs had hanged herself from the old olive tree in her home village; she wore the orange floral dress of happier days. Mitry had gradually faded away as he had lived, accumulating words and knowledge. Farid had taken off in his four poster bed; a generous host, he had let out a welcoming cry:

'Come in, beautiful! Make yourself at home, I was expecting you!'

Endowing death with beauty, femininity, made his departure triumphant. He went quickly towards it as if embarking on a new love affair. Slimane, who had never been bothered by Farid's moods and eccentricity, sobbed at his bedside. Odette and her children, who had come at once from the various corners of the world, also wept.

*

Kalya trembles for Sybil and turns round. In the doorway, the little girl waves her arms to reassure her.

Kalya again repeats the gesture of pushing her back to make it clear that she is not to leave her post at any price. The sight of the child waving her arms and taking a few steps backwards, as if she senses her grandmother's anxiety, soothes her.

If only it could all begin again. If the film could be rewound. Myriam and Ammal would still be walking, moving forward. Their clothes vivid.

Around the two young women, the pool of blood spreads wider and wider...

TWELVE

Ammal and Myriam had just dropped Kalya and the little girl in front of the steps of the Grand Hôtel at Solar. Then they drove off in the white Peugeot.

Without Sybil chattering or Kalya enthusing about this and that, the journey back to town seemed dull. The branches on the trees were covered with a dark sheen. A cloudless but heavy sky hung over the mountainside. At each bend, the blue of the sea took on a green tinge. Insects were crushed, splattered against the windscreen.

'I'm thirsty.'

Ammal braked. They walked towards the spring hidden between the burning rocks. The water tasted bitter. With both hands, they splashed water over their hair, their foreheads, their necks and under their arms. Then they tried to console each other, to find reasons for hope, to tell each other that the recent atrocities would be the last.

Their words flowed haltingly, no sooner uttered than reduced to dust. All that remained was the certainty of their friendship.

*

Late July 1975; the Grand Hôtel had changed. It was almost empty; most of the guests who had once spent their summers there now went to Europe. It had lost some of its glory; its façade was slowly falling into decay.

The previous manager, the plump Gabriel, was long since dead, and had been replaced by an Italian with nervous features, a polite smile and a diploma in hotel management. He wore dark glasses and his forty years to striking effect.

The tables, the parasols and the garden chairs had faded. The oleander hedge had doubled in size, as had the weeping willow. Beds of nasturtiums surrounded the lawn. Large sandy paving stones replaced the gravel path.

Sybil joined a group of children around the swing. They were making a commotion, playing with their brightly coloured ball, chasing one another and shrieking. A boy grabbed Sybil's dress and would not let go. She struggled, broke free and ran around the tables, brushing past her grandmother.

'He won't catch me!'

The little boy caught her by the gate. She fought with ever diminishing conviction. Kalya watched them head back towards the others, having made their peace, hand in hand.

Standing on the swing, facing each other, they rose up together bending their knees in unison. High, higher and higher. Their faces, bathed in perspiration, touched each other, lit up. The ropes were taut to breaking point.

'Aren't you afraid?'

'I'm never afraid.'

'What's your name?'

'Sybil.'

'That's a funny name!'

'What's yours?'

'Samyr. With a "y".'

'Mine's with a "y" too!'

*

The room that Kalya and Sybil shared was not the one used by Nouza. It had the same curtains of cretonne cotton and over-looked the same pine wood, but the balcony was much smaller. The little girl let herself fall backwards onto the bed.

'Kalya, I love this country. I'm going to come back every year.'

She fell asleep fully dressed, a smile on her lips. The light from the lamps in the garden gave her hair an even richer shine. Kalya covered the child with her coat and kissed her hands.

*

Night gradually descended, bringing its shadows.

The words of concern exchanged in a low voice by Myriam and Ammal, who were still in the car, penetrated the room and floated above the child's bed.

From the bottom of the garden, a shrill screeching could be heard.

X

'I loathe bats! Sometimes they screech at night, fly into your room and get caught in your hair! If you switch the light on, do make sure you close the windows, Kalya,' urges my grandmother.

After a long walk with Anaïs, I have dozed off, fully dressed, on the mauve bedspread. On the verandah, Nouza, Odette and Mitry sit around a bridge table, talking in low voices. Although the curtains are drawn, I can make out the three shadows and can hear their coffee cups chink against the saucers.

From time to time, Nouza comes into the room and leans over me.

'Do you need anything, Kalya? Are you asleep?'

'Yes, yes, I'm asleep.'

Her laugh rings out in the warm night. She takes hold of my hand and showers my palm with kisses. Then she goes off again to join the others.

My great-uncle Farid left as suddenly as he had arrived. Since his departure, a calm rhythm has returned. Odette, his willing victim, looks less distracted; she prattles on with no one to say:

'What are you talking about, nobody's interested in that,' every time she opens her mouth.

Mitry looks less forlorn, has taken to adding a few drops of alcohol to his coffee, and seems more considerate.

Nouza is boasting about her latest exploits at poker and is trying to teach Odette bridge.

'It's too complicated, Nouza. You've got brains, I haven't.'

She preferred backgammon, which she used to play with

Mitry. Everywhere he goes he takes with him a box inlaid with mother-of-pearl, which he inherited from his father. He never takes off his cotton gloves, not even to move the counters and the die.

Since he does not talk about his own poetry – although tempted to show a few pages to Nicolas, he always restrained himself for fear of disappointing him – Mitry recites at length the poets he admires: Shakespeare, Ibn Al Roumi, Hugo, Lamartine, Musset, Al Moutanabbi, Chawqui.

Odette is enraptured by it. My grandmother, impatient, is already onto her eighth cigarette.

The day draws to a close, the hours fall one by one. Because of the flying insects, they haven't lit the lamp yet. Nouza comes back into my room to empty the ashtray.

I sit up and switch on the bedside light:

'Is it late?'

She smiles. Late! Why late? For whom? The word means nothing. Life is long, all encompassing, why calculate, why hurry? What is there to catch up with? There is no threat hanging over them. The summer will be long, no conflict, no war will interrupt it. Man's folly is all elsewhere, far away. 'An oasis!' repeated Farid. 'We were born in a Garden of Eden! At least, in our land we can be certain of dying of natural causes!'

*

I am terribly impatient. I wish I could go away, be somewhere else. Although I love Nouza, I find her laziness and her clear gaze disconcerting. I want to grow up, clear out, live differently, feel differently. Open my eyes until they burn.

The plaintive barking of the hotel dog strains against the moon. Something haggard, something faded in my grandmother's face moves me.

I make her sit down on the divan. I remove her make-up. She yawns and lets me do as I please.

I take her nightdress out of the wardrobe. I come back to her. I take off her shoes and her stockings. I undress her like a child.

THIRTEEN

In town, things were hotting up. Rumours of brawls and other acts of violence had reached the Grand Hôtel.

Odette was trying to reassure us on the phone, maintaining that they were merely isolated incidents. We just had to stay calm, order would soon be restored.

And so, after a week, Mario drove up to Solar to bring Sybil and her grandmother back to town. Kalya wondered whether the news had appeared in the foreign press. But the little girl's parents, who were travelling in the bush, were out of reach. At least that way they would be spared any anxiety about the child. She would be back before them.

*

Sybil took her leave from her friends and Samyr on the steps of the hotel. It was late afternoon. The garden was almost deserted, except for the tennis court where four youths were exchanging clumsy shots in the faltering light.

'I'm leaving tomorrow too,' said Samyr.

He slipped a matchbox into her hand. Inside it was a piece of string in the shape of a ring.

She promised to see him again in town in a few days time. They would go to the beach together.

Mario had a tight grip on the steering wheel. He explained why he had come – he thought it was better to return before the roads were closed.

'Has it already happened?'

'Not yet. But we've just had power cuts. That has never happened before either.'

As they drove down, the daylight was fading fast. The pale beam of the headlights swept the foot of the cliffs, which had been shored up with stone walls. In the depths of the valleys, they caught an occasional glimpse of the capital, all lit up.

Mario strained his eyes, and spoke in a breathless voice. He could not conceal his fears for the country, for his children. Georges was an ardent militant in one party. Myriam and Ammal, ever the utopians, were trying to bring all the communities together.

Both were a source of worry to him. He was distressed by their arguments. Alarmed by an expression of scorn on his son's face or by an outburst of anger from his daughter, he wondered how to ward off the impending tragedy. His words fell on deaf ears and only stirred up their quarrel all the more.

'Is it war?' asked Sybil.

She talked of war as though it were a film, images with no reality. She repeated:

'Will there be a war? A real war?'

Kalya remained silent. Mario tried to get out of an awkward situation:

'You'll be leaving, Sybil. You'll spend the rest of the holidays at your grandmother's. In her country.'

'I want to stay. Go on, Kalya, can we stay? At least a few days longer.'

Kalya placed her hand on Mario's arm:

'It can't be that serious?'

He went on without conviction:

'Perhaps not.'

*

Some streets were closed off. They drove round several blocks before reaching Odette's.

At the foot of the stairs they met Myriam. She was in a hurry and bumped into her father without recognizing him. He caught her and placed his hands on her shoulders:

'Where are you going?'

She spoke hurriedly of car bombs, of kidnapping, of vendettas.

'Who is responsible?'

'We don't know. Nobody knows who's to blame. Each side blames the other.'

Myriam went over to Kalya, who was surprised by the concern that she showed.

'We're going to try to do something. If you're still here, I'll keep you posted.'

She leaned over and kissed Sybil.

'But leave if you can. Leave as soon as possible.'

'I don't want to leave,' replied the child.

The next day, all flights out were cancelled. Sporadic fighting had burst out around the runways, so they had had to close the airport. The authorities stated that these measures were temporary. The population believed they were, too.

*

Odette was waiting for them, surrounded by her knick-knacks. In the illuminated display cabinets, opaline glassware shone brightly.

Slimane was laying the table and softly humming a tune he remembered from his childhood. He was watching them out of the corner of his eye.

The little girl went over to him:

'What are you singing?'

'I can teach it to you if you like.'

'Yes, yes.'

'After me, then:'

Water goes, water comes
As parched as hunger
And gentler than the heart.

Sybil sang after him.

'You learn very fast!'

'Where's my tortoise?'

Slimane showed her the shoe box. He had looked after everything. Julius was not short of water or lettuce.

Mario left. As soon as he had gone, Odette began to fire off questions at her niece:

'How was the hotel, Kalya? What about the manager? He's funny, isn't he? Did you have the same room? And the mirrors in the foyer? Did you see, they've removed nearly all of them! And did you see what they've replaced the marble in the gaming room with? And the gravel paths, don't you think those sandy paving stones are dreadful?'.

The incidents of the last few days did not seem to have affected her.

Kalya's curt replies did not satisfy her. Kalya would have liked to add that she had never liked the Grand Hôtel, nor its stucco décor, and that she had only gone back there because of Nouza.

Odette was miffed by Kalya's response:

'Haven't you got anything to tell me?'

'It wasn't long enough.'

She persisted, asking what she thought of the new manager:

'Why does he always wear dark glasses? Anyone would think he had something to hide. You don't know either? Times have changed, whatever happened to the good old days? Where are Nouza, Farid and Mitry?'

She emphasized each name, as though she wanted to engrave them on her heart. She sighed, remembered Gabriel, his talents as a chef, his weakness for cabaret dancers. Then she smiled to herself as she recalled Farid's escapades:

'Your uncle was such a character! What a long time ago all that was!'

Slimane finished laying the table. On hearing Farid's name uttered, he turned his face to us and gave a nod of agreement.

The night was the colour of amber. The illuminated display cabinets gave the drawing room an unreal air.

Odette said a few personal things about Mitry, who until that summer had been but a pale shadow in her life.

'It's a long time ago, lost in the mists of time!'

XI

Nouza is dozing on the divan. I gaze at her as though she were my granddaughter.

The tortoiseshell combs have slipped out of her hair. It is hardly grey at all, and tumbles around her face. Her face is relaxed, its wrinkles softened. Her round shoulders and her gazelle-like neck offer themselves to the night. I would like to photograph her, keep her like this for ever. My eyes aren't enough. Nor is my memory.

I resolve to buy myself a camera to capture all those moments that I love and keep them alive. Although I am only twelve, I think about old age, of that decay which lies in wait, of those stooped, frail bodies that the earth will swallow up one day. Nouza bears the marks of her years, but I cannot imagine her really ravaged by time. Far less gone, no more.

Nor can I imagine finding her in another world. What form would this other world take? In what guise would Nouza appear to me? Would she be my grandmother or would she be Nouza as a young girl, or even Nouza as a child?

I would have to get a camera quickly, before she aged even more, even before I could afford to pay for it myself.

As soon as I had one, I would photograph my grandmother from all angles: in the evening, in her diamanté dress; in the morning, leaning against the balustrade on the balcony. I would catch her unawares, smiling and winking, with that wayward strand of hair that made her look mischievous. With those arms that opened to greet me:

'Come, my little Kalya, I like it when you're here.'

*

The shadows of Mitry and Odette stamp themselves on the curtain that is between me and the verandah. I switch off the light in the room for my grandmother to sleep. I tiptoe across the room and draw back a corner of the curtain, I peep through the netting.

Outside, the gas lamps in the garden flicker. A faint light falls onto the backgammon box which lies open between the two players. I glimpse the dice cup in its red case and the black and white counters. I recognize Mitry's gloved hand and Odette's hand with its crimson nails resting on the side of the box.

Mitry's voice soars melodiously, reciting the words of a poem. I cannot make out the words but I like their sound.

The brown cotton glove fascinates me. It no longer throws the die, it no longer moves the counters, it inches towards Odette's naked hand. I shouldn't be there, but I remain rooted to the spot, mesmerized, fearing the worst: Odette crying in outrage; Nouza waking with a start.

Quite the opposite happened.

The gloved hand finally touched her fingers. Hesitant. She seized it and squeezed it passionately.

I was ashamed of being there and seeing it all. I put the curtain back in place and withdrew into the room. Nouza awoke and called out:

'I'm going back to my own bed. Aren't you in bed yet, Kalya?'

She rubbed her eyes with her index fingers, like a cat moistening its lips with the tip of its tongue.

'Grandma, do you know what I'd like for my thirteenth birthday?'

'Tell me and you shall have it.'

'A camera.'

She did not wait for my birthday. A few days later, she slipped over my shoulder a red leather case containing a Kodak.

FOURTEEN

A series of explosions went off in various parts of the capital. It was, apparently, the work of a few irresponsible people of whom there were no traces. Then followed a few days of calm, but the airport was not reopened.

The city seemed to be on the threshold of a drama, whose consequences were quite unpredictable. People convinced one another that tacit compromises between the unknown protagonists would restore order and bring harmony to the different communities. For such optimists, people who believed in happiness, each sign of appeasement encouraged them to forget; to return, with confidence, to their daily lives.

*

In Odette's district, the bazaar with the scarlet shop front was the first to be blown to pieces. The store was to the left of the square. Sybil often went there. From when she was small, she had been used to doing the shopping, and Odette and Kalya had just given her permission to run a few errands instead of Slimane.

The shopkeeper, Aziz, was a man loved by all, with his chubby face and round eyes. Several times a day, he would stop what he was doing as soon as he heard the muezzin's call, and pray. He wore a brown skullcap on his bald head and took great care of the thick moustache that drooped on either side of his mouth.

Aziz took pride in proving to his new customers – the old ones were already convinced – that you could find anything and everything in his booth! The little girl had great fun asking him for some unusual item, just to see if he had it: a yo-yo, a scoobeedoo, a Beatles record or a carnival mask. In less than a minute, he would pull the object out from an indescribable jumble of things and hold it up triumphantly.

'Stamps, newspapers, magazines – in three languages – tooth-paste, chewing-gum, polishes, beer, paper handkerchiefs, ciga-rettes, beauty creams, whisky and tambourines, needles, balls of wool, toys, balloons, aspirin... You can ask for anything you want, since I've got it all!'

This list filled him with joy, and he could have gone on for hours, punctuating it with the word 'since'. 'Since' constantly recurred in his speech, as if a relation between cause and effect gave his existence coherence and linked together the numerous and assorted objects that filled his tiny shop.

The shopkeeper pulled at the huge drawer of a dilapidated chest but it was jammed. His arms taut, he pulled again. There were beads of sweat on his brow and on the fuzzy black hair that his unbuttoned, brightly coloured shirt revealed.

'Drawer of the devil, open, since I command you to do so!'

It gave way so suddenly that he fell over backwards, waving his arms and legs in the air. Sybil could barely suppress her laughter.

'Laugh! Don't be ashamed to laugh since it's funny and since I haven't broken any bones!'

He laughed at it too. She helped him up. He finally took a little inlaid box out of the drawer, which was crammed full of cheap knick-knacks. He lifted the lid and it played a shrill tune to which Aziz hummed dreamily.

'It's a song from Paris.'

'Have you been to Paris?'

'One day, I'll travel too! On the day Paris was liberated, the crowd sang and clapped. Here in this square. You weren't born then. Do me a favour, take this box, it's for you. For your grand-mother, take this bunch of grapes. She'll remember their unique taste! She'll let you taste them. Is your grandmother from here?'

'Not exactly. Her grandparents went to Egypt, more than a hundred years ago. She lives in Europe.'

'What about you? You've got a different accent.'

'I'm from America.'

'USA, OK, Pepsi-Coca-Cola! I know! But you still have traces of your origins in your blood, even though you don't know it.'

'Do you think so? Ah! I'd like that!'

She clapped her hands.

'I am happy, happy!'

'You like here?'

'I love it..'

This place was a real treasure trove and Aziz was a magician, so different from the hurried shopkeepers back at home. Despite the comings and goings of his customers, he always had time for Sybil, helping her to fill her bag and asking after Odette and Kalya.

The little girl often chose siesta time to go to the deserted shop. She would come across the shopkeeper snoozing on the counter or on the floor, leaning up against a sack of flour or rice. She would sit down beside him. They would jabber on for an hour and more, skipping from one language to another, waving their hands about and laughing.

*

It was a few days later, during the siesta, that the explosion occurred.

Before Odette or Kalya could stop her, the little girl tore downstairs and rushed towards the shop. Smoke billowed out.

Her hands pressed against what remained of the window, squashing her face up against the dusty glass, she had trouble making out, and then recognizing Aziz's body. A soft, bloody, inert mass, slumped over the counter.

She went in, with searing heart.

117

The shelves, heavily laden, had collapsed onto a heap of rubble. Bits of wooden beams and old iron were mixed in with the debris.

Sybil approached the body. It was a nightmare, a horror film.

A crowd of local people had gathered in the square. Some, followed by Aziz's screaming parents, entered the shop through the gaping openings.

The little girl refused to believe what she saw. She wanted to touch her friend, wake him up. It was like one of those serials where the body, which is never completely dead, comes to life again the next day for the start of a new episode. She was convinced that Aziz would get up and once again take his place in his rebuilt shop. She could hear him already:

'It was a joke! Since I frightened you, you're entitled to a free Coca-Cola and some Suchard chocolate.'

Sybil had never encountered death, real death. In her country, death took place elsewhere; well out of sight, in hospital beds, in plane or car crashes. Bodies returned to air, or discreetly disappeared into varnished wooden coffins.

*

That very morning, Sybil had bought some things from Aziz. On leaving the shop, she had turned round in the doorway to say goodbye once more. He had been holding his tiny pink cup and was sipping his syrupy coffee with delight. He had called out:

'See you tomorrow, God willing!'

God had not been willing. She stretched out her hands to touch his shoulder. Was that face really his? That bloody mask sprinkled with sand. Its skull was cracked, its mouth grimaced and its mischievous eyes were dull and motionless.

Despite her revulsion, she drew even nearer. She placed her hand on the back of her friend's neck, and gently tapped it as if to console him for having become that repulsive, grotesque thing, and to promise him, in their private language, never to forget him. Neither him, nor his country. Nor death. Ever.

*

When, shortly afterwards, Kalya pulled her away, trying to shield her from the sight, she resisted.

'Not yet.'

A furry rabbit slid off one of the shelves, and landed on the counter. The impact set off its clockwork mechanism. The animal cheerfully began to beat its drum, brushing the shopkeeper's head several times.

The crowd jostled with ambulancemen and policemen around the store. A throng of people explaining and shouting. Where had the explosion come from? Had Aziz belonged to a clandestine organization? Nothing made sense. Suspicions were voiced. Passions and qualms spread insidiously.

XII

The first death I witnessed was that of my grandfather.

The family doctor, a distant cousin, had announced with solemnity and tact that his days were numbered. Nicolas was grateful to him for keeping his promise to keep nothing from him. Since fate had been generous enough to allow him to die in his bed, he insisted on looking death in the face, convinced that it was a matter of the greatest importance.

*

Summer was drawing to a close. The family was scattered through France and Italy, travelling from the mountains to their spa towns. By chance, I happened to be there, which seemed to please my grandfather. Despite my young age, he wanted to prepare me for the idea of death, of loss.

Some time earlier, I had talked to him about it, rejecting the idea that life just comes to an end, that life, which is so short anyway, could be taken from us, though we have no say over our entrance or our exit. He never forgot this or the vehemence with which I argued.

He realized that this problem continued to trouble me, and tried to find a way of presenting the inescapable end to me as fulfilment rather than loss. He tried to persuade me that to accept mortality gave each event its true weight, making some more substantial, some lighter:

'In the face of death, it doesn't carry much weight!' he would sometimes say to me.

And on other occasions:

120

'What joy each crumb of happiness when you know that everything must end!'

In his opinion, such an attitude towards destiny would help
me live. He was not mistaken.

*

I never knew what my grandfather thought about the afterlife. He
did not seem worried about it. It was as though such a situation
was beyond the realm of the imagination, outside his scope. He
did not wish to delude himself, but left the doors open. He could
see, without reservation, the validity of all beliefs, as long as they
were not barricaded behind walls, surrounded with barbed wire
and hostile to others.

Nicolas had prepared for his death. He organized it so as to
spare his family the sight of his deterioration and his suffering.
To help him on his way and to get over the worst of the death
pangs, he requested only the help of the cook, Constantin, his
staunch helmsman. With the help of the kitchen boy, he was to
tidy everything after Nicolas's death, before Nouza and I came
into the little room.

'Constantin, let Kalya come in. It is good for her to know what
is important, and that departing is easy. These things worry her.'

*

I can still see my grandfather in his camp bed, laid out on the
cotton bedspread in his suit of raw silk. The sun filtered in
through the half-open shutters. Two fans made the curtains
billow like sails.

His smooth, calm face was smiling at us. His smile remote or
immediate, depending on how the light fell.

Nouza sobbing, found letters for each of us on the bedside
table. Nicolas wrote that he considered himself fulfilled to have

reached the best years of life (in his day, to reach sixty was an achievement); that he felt privileged to have lived, with his family, far from the horrors of war, of civil strife, of deportation. He asked them for joy rather than tears.

Mitry remained prostrate at the foot of the bed. That evening, he placed a few sheets of poems dedicated to Nicolas – some of those that he had never dared read to him – on the corner of the pillow. They were put in the coffin.

I added a ring adorned with a turquoise scarab, to which I was greatly attached.

*

Farid turned up the next day, fuming against his sister who had not contacted him in time.

'My only brother-in-law! The best of men! I loved him, I loved him. I adored him!'

Odette had not yet entered our lives.

FIFTEEN

The explosion was followed by a lull. In the newspapers and on the radio, they repeatedly issued reassuring statements.

'Just an accident,' maintained Odette. 'I told you, Kalya, it was a leak in a gas cylinder which caused all that damage in the bazaar. All right, it does happen that people botch things here, that they're negligent, careless, quick-tempered; but we're not mad! Nobody wants a catastrophe. We enjoy life, we all enjoy life! You have nothing to fear. You and the child can stay until the end of your vacation. We can go up to the mountains for a week before you leave. This time, I'll come with you.'

*

Using scaffolding and hoarding, the workmen covered up the gaping hole in the store. Posters extolling Elizabeth Arden products, washing powders, Black and White whisky, TWA, Air France, Air India and MEA airlines or archaeological sites were pasted across the façade.

'The airport will open soon.'

Sybil begged her grandmother to stay a few more days. She wanted to see her friends from the Grand Hôtel again, swim with Samyr, ask questions of Myriam.

'Perhaps I'll never come back. Let me stay a little longer.'

Aziz's violent death had distressed her deeply. Every day, she would walk past the new hoarding, run her hand over the pictures on the advertisements and the rough wood; peer inside through the holes.

The store had been emptied and cleaned. Around the huge empty space, great iron girders held up the walls and ceiling. From the depths of this cavity it seemed at times to Sybil that her friend was teetering towards her, his arms filled with piles of knick-knacks.

'I must hurry. Put everything back, otherwise I'll lose all my customers. Come and help me, little one.'

The emptiness disoriented him. Aziz cast about him distraught.

'I've still got hundreds of things in stock. Let's be quick, before the customers arrive.'

Sybil restrained herself from pointing out that he was dead. He stopped swaying, took a breath and, spoke to her once more:

'Come here.'

She went closer, pretending to believe in his existence.

'Since you haven't forgotten me, Sybil, take the cap from my head. That's my present for this morning. I'm giving it to you in memory.'

*

Through the loose planks in the fence, Sybil had just spotted the storekeeper's brown skullcap under a heap of rubble. She slipped her arm through the gap and grasped a piece of the woolly material between her thumb and forefinger. Pulling it towards her, raising clouds of dust.

The cap in her hands at last. She clutched it to her chest, then began to run towards the apartment block.

She raced up the stairs four at a time and bumped into Odette in the living room.

'Where have you been, Sybil?'

'Outside.'

'You're always outside.'

She did not reply but abruptly left the room and shut herself in her room.

Sybil pulled her kitbag from the bottom of the wardrobe. Right at the bottom she gently placed the partially charred skullcap and covered it with a few tissues.

She would take it with her. Everywhere.

*

Mario avoided talking about the events when he visited his neighbours. Despite the distress caused him by his children, whose disagreements simply intensified, he convinced himself that their quarrels were childish and would be over the next day.

*

One morning, Georges rang at the door and took Kalya to one side. When they were alone, he took a revolver from his pocket and gave it to her.

'It's for you.'

'For me?'

'Odette is too old. Slimane wouldn't be able to use it. In this country, one should not remain unarmed.'

'I don't understand.'

'Anything could erupt.'

'Your father thinks...'

'It suits my father not to see anything.'

His index finger looped around the trigger-guard, Georges swung the pistol back and forth.

'I'll explain how it works.'

'I'll never use a gun.'

'Would you allow yourself to be murdered? You and your family, and not do anything about it?'

125

'Murdered? Why? By whom?'

'You come from elsewhere, that's obvious! You can't understand what's happening here, there's no place for your old-
fashioned humanism here. The hope of uniting us all causes
nothing but tension. Look at history! Fine ideas aren't enough,
gathering different people in one place gives rise to hatred. Do
I shock you? You are like Myriam, like Ammal. Think what you
like, but I'm leaving you this gun.'

Despite Kalya's refusal, he went over each part of the revolver
and showed her how it worked:

'Here's the trigger and above it, the safety catch. You release
the cylinder by squeezing this catch.'

'I've already told you, I'll never use a gun.'

'And if the child were in danger? You wouldn't say that then.'

He told her about the street fights he had just been involved
in.

'I've got one piece of advice for you: leave with Sybil as soon as
possible. Meanwhile, protect yourself. There's nothing unusual in
having a gun in the house. Everyone has one in this country.'

Georges opened the chest of drawers and slipped the revolver
in between the tablemats.

XIII

'Come over here, Nouza, I have a present for you.'

The day after my great-uncle's arrival, we were in the lobby of the Grand Hôtel, on our way to the dining room. After the scene the previous day, the manager had reserved the best table for us, by the French windows overlooking the garden. Gabriel himself had supervised the floral decoration.

Farid, with a mysterious air, led his sister over to the furthest corner of the room. Odette followed. My uncle begged her, in a tone that brooked no argument, to leave him alone with his sister. No doubt he had some family business to settle. His wife drew back.

I was there too. My great-uncle had not yet assigned me my part. Nouza took the initiative and declared:

'Kalya, you stay with us.'

This performance was just another of his whims, and my grandmother knew how much I would enjoy unwrapping the parcel, discovering the surprise. Farid did not dare contradict her; he treated me, depending on the time and the place, either as a carefree kid or as a responsible young girl who could be let in on a secret.

We were standing in the quietest corner of the lobby. Farid placed the parcel on the corner table which was covered in a midnight blue velvet cloth. He adopted a serious air.

'Nouza, open this parcel.'

'Let Kalya open it.'

The lamp was covered by a pleated rosewood taffeta lampshade,
which was fringed with matching tassels, and gave out an iridescent light which suffused the mysterious object.

127

Farid glanced around to make sure that there was nobody in the vicinity. Then he commanded:

'Go on, Kalya!'

I prolonged the pleasure, unwrapping the parcel in my own time. First, the scarlet silk ribbon: I wound it round my finger and tied a knot in it before throwing it on the floor.

'You'll never guess what it is,' breathed my great-uncle in his sister's ear.

I tackled the glazed paper printed with golden stars. Then I removed several layers of tissue paper: I was enchanted with the rustling. My great-uncle did not take his eyes off his sister, waiting for the final effect.

At last, his cheeks burning, he removed his glasses and rubbed the lenses with a monogrammed handkerchief.

'I'm sure it's the first time you'll have seen such a thing.'

I reached for the leather covered box.

'May I keep the box, Grandma?'

'Of course you can have it.'

Heaps of paper were strewn over the floor. Impatience was overtaking us, but I prolonged the wait. The last sheet of paper had a subtle velvet feel. I stroked it with my fingers. Unable to contain himself, my great-uncle snatched the present from my hands.

'Close your eyes, both of you.'

He took off the last of the wrapping and placed the present on the velvet where it could be clearly seen, in the bright shaft of light.

'Now, open your eyes both of you. Look!'

*

My grandmother's surprise was equalled only by Farid's delighted expression.

'It's a jewel, a real jewel! It used to belong to a sultan.'

He picked it up and held it out to her. Nouza flinched and hid her hands behind her back.

'I'll never touch it!'

It was a little revolver which looked like a toy, with a mother-of-pearl butt and a silver barrel and trigger.

'Why are you giving me this, Farid?'

'To protect you.'

'Protect me from what?'

'You are forgetting what happened at your neighbours; barely six months ago.'

Nouza shivered. With a wink, she reminded him that I was present.

'Don't talk to me about that.'

He went on:

'Poor Antoine would have defended himself if only he had had a gun. He went to his assassins like a lamb to the slaughter. Olga was dragged from between the sheets, gagged, chloroformed and pushed under the bed. They stabbed her husband to death, right above her head.'

'Enough, please!'

'You think it only happens to others! When I'm far away, I think of you. There has been no man in the house since Nicolas died!'

'There's Mitry...'

He shrugged and refrained from comment. Mitry had no place among the ranks of real men. A pen-pusher who wore cotton gloves!

Farid took some tiny bullets out of his pocket and loaded them in the magazine.

'I'll teach you how to use it. It's a lady's pistol. But it's effective.'

'I don't want it.'

Her brother put the present back in his pocket, looking contrite. He tried to give the impression of being composed. He took his glasses off and put them back on several times; took his cigarette case out of his pocket and, finding it empty, cursed Odette's slovenliness.

Finally, he grasped his sister's hand and brought it to his lips.

'As you wish, darling. A protective measure, that's all.'

Before leaving us, he absent-mindedly stroked my hair.

'Don't worry, Kalya, we'll find another way of protecting your grandmother.'

He kicked the pile of paper that had amassed at the foot of the corner table:

'What a mess!' and strode over towards his wife.

At the other end of the lobby sat Odette, a silk shawl drawn tightly round her shoulders. She was knitting a loose-stitch bed jacket for her sister-in-law Nouza who would never wear it.

*

I found out later that two men had broken into Nouza's neighbours' house at night to burgle them. The couple were asleep but the noise had awoken Antoine. In the dark, he thought he recognized the voice of the chauffeur.

'Vittorio, is that you? Vittorio!'

One of them flew at him and overcame him, while the other chloroformed his wife, tied her up and pushed her under the bed.

The stolen watch had a cover which was initialled and inlaid with small rubies. The murderers were soon traced.

During the trial, Olga wore a long widow's veil. Buxom and jolly, she had to clear herself at length from a terrible accusation of complicity. The newspapers made a meal of it and many friends became distant.

Although her innocence was established, Olga never got over it. Her eyes darted about like caged birds, her head was bowed. Her face had grown hard, white as chalk.

SIXTEEN

An evil circle gradually surrounded the town. The walls were covered in graffiti. There was talk of more murders, more kidnappings. Arms of all sizes began to appear. Weapons of war, tanks and jeeps with cannons rose from the bowels of the earth. A few shells were fired. Children went up to the top floors of the tall buildings to follow the tracer bullets and see the flashes of gunfire. It looked like a firework display – fear had not yet made its presence felt.

A few days later, Georges had been seen at the wheel of his Fiat near the Diana cinema. A group of men barred his path. They got into the car with him and pushed him to one side, a revolver at the back of his neck. One of them had taken his place in the driver's seat.

The car drove off at speed. A few hours later, it was found, intact, in a ditch. But Georges had disappeared.

Mario telephoned everywhere, raced here and there, trying to pick up a lead, find out who had kidnapped his son and how best to negotiate his release.

Despite his outward calm, his hands shook and he hid them behind his back. The veins in his neck and temples stood out.

*

Ammal and Myriam decided to bring forward the date of their meeting. A movement such as theirs, without the backing of guns or manifestoes, has to establish itself quickly.

Georges' disappearance had shattered them. In the face of danger, of indiscriminate violence, differences had to be forgotten.

They had to find Georges at all costs, and convince him that no doctrine, or religion should determine how people related to one another; that partisan struggles were genocidal, and would only result in a spiral of disaster.

They thought that they could count on Kalya and explained the plan of action to her. As soon as they had met up in the centre of the square, each would wave her yellow scarf, that bright symbol of unity, of peace. Lookouts positioned around the square would spread the news. It would travel from mouth to mouth. People would shout it to their friends, they in turn to their own friends.

The waiting crowds would start walking: some of the people would wave their scarves over the heads of the throng. They would invade the five streets and the few winding alleys that led to the square. Then they would all converge on the centre. Transcending adherence to different creeds and clans, faiths and ideology, their voices would awaken the voices of silence, dispel all fears and change those unspoken words into a single word of agreement, of freedom. One word for everyone.

'We shouldn't wait any longer, it will be tomorrow.'

*

It will be tomorrow. It is already today.

Any second now, dawn will break over the square. Kalya has lost the sweet habit of expecting a sunny day.

It is dark in Odette's apartment. She opens the shutters of her bedroom. Later, she will come and rest her elbows on the window sill to watch the two young women meet, and then the arrival of the crowd.

Kalya rummages in her suitcase for a light coloured scarf to match theirs, but she cannot find one. Later, she will ask Odette for one. They will wave them from the window before they go down to join the crowd.

White, fluorescent streaks filter through the slight gaps in the cloth of night.

Kalya slept well, despite the excitement of the previous day.

'You'll be able to see us from here. Ammal will arrive from the alley opposite and I'll come from the one that runs alongside our apartment block. If you lean out, you'll be able to see me.'

Myriam showed her the two places and pointed out the whole route, emphasizing the rhythm of their footsteps by tapping her wrist: they will be slow, measured, solemn steps. Then her hands joined, her fingers intertwined to denote their union.

'Don't move until we have met up, wait for the scarf signal. Only then, telephone this number. Those who live further away will be waiting for your call.'

She gave Kalya a scrap of paper rolled into a ball on which she had written the six figures.

'After a quarter of an hour, you can come downstairs with Sybil.'

'With Sybil?'

'You'll have nothing to fear. Our message will have reached hundreds of people. Everything is finalized. There will be a huge gathering. The square will soon be bursting with people. Then, before the sectarian killings can start, the crowd will flood the town like a raging torrent. I would like you to be with us, Kalya.'

She felt closer to her than ever before.

'Come and join us with the child. It will be a great day for Sybil. A day to remember.'

Kalya pictured herself mingling with the surging crowd, holding Sybil's hand. A day to remember, indeed.

'We've brought the date forward, we had to act quickly, before...'

'Before what?'

Myriam did not finish her sentence.

Kalya persisted:

'Before what?'

As if she feared that doubt might set in and undermine her strength, the young woman cut her short:

'See you tomorrow, Kalya. It's good to know that you are there, at your window, watching over us.'

*

Odette is in the living room, facing the verandah overlooking the sea. She is sunk in her easy chair, also awaiting daybreak.

In the adjacent kitchen, Slimane is preparing her breakfast. Every morning for forty years, he has made it with a care that had not been spoiled by habit. The smell of coffee and toast wafts into the room.

Odette does not know about the meeting. She would have refused to listen to the 'groundless rumours', to be taken in by the 'lies you read in the press'. She would have found the young women's plan provocative, useless. She would have tried to stop them.

At the other end of the apartment, Kalya is leaning out of the window overlooking the square. At times, she can sense a vague threat hanging over the open space. Her heart stops. She presses her hand against her breast, and prays that her beating heart will remain calm.

*

Slimane brings in two packs of playing cards on the silver breakfast tray. Odette is very fond of playing patience. Often, during the morning, he would stand behind her and advise her to turn over one card rather than another, or point out a set she had not noticed.

'You are right, Slimane, I'm so scatty! Here, what do you think? Shall I play the black one or the red?'

Soon, the sun will pour down onto the roofs and terraces, soak into the walls, into the ground. The sky will turn a liquid blue first, then, gradually, white hot and then acquire the consistency of stone.

The deserted square looks like an arena, a white page. Anything can be written on it, before...

'Before. Before. Before.'

Kalya catches herself repeating Myriam's words. She finds it curious that she had stumbled on that little word: 'Before.'

*

Ammal has just appeared on the far side. A yellow blob, a line, a sketch. As she walks, her scarf, her dress and her espadrilles grow more distinct.

'We will appear from either side of the square at the same time.'

Kalya rests her chest on the window sill and leans out. At the foot of the building, Myriam has just appeared from a nearby alleyway.

'Hurry, before...'

...before the town is divided before the last alley is blocked before hostages become common currency before murders and revenge before rival militias swarm over the city and fight each other before the first the second the third round before the mutinies the factions the clashes before the armies from here and elsewhere pound loot terrify before ceasefire follows ceasefire to no avail and refugees take to the roads in search of their home villages before the villages are taken over by pillagers before snipers shoot down their victims before leaders form alliances attack each other and are reconciled only to fight again before the enemy is discovered in the house next door before this morning's friend becomes this evening's executioner before informers multiply before cynical truces before roads paths and boulevards bristle with the roar of deadly machines before bazookas mortars Katioucha rocket launchers 357 magnum guns with 106 Kalashnikov rockets Sol-Sol missiles and bazookas become everyday words before the assassination of leaders and the massacre of innocent people before the buildings collapse and the bodies burn and break before the grass and the earth are drenched in blood before mothers scream with pain and children are scarred for life before the people flee this murderous and murdered land in hundreds before equilibrium gives way and the eternal puppet master tangles the strings and collapses in a heap of pulleys canvas and rigging among his dislocated puppets before the miracle-acrobat symbol of this city defeated by too many plots too many storms teeters and falls from its rope before the worst becomes the daily diet before the dam of all brotherhood and discussion bursts and

horror devastates and floods before before before before before before...

*

Before is already no longer. While Kalya moves from one point in the square to another, there is nothing left but the after.

In front of her, it is no longer the emptiness of the blank page. The page is sullied, splattered. The pool of blood spreads.

With every footstep she draws a tenuous, fragile line. A line which starts at the doorway where Sybil is standing and leads to the centre of the square where these two bodies are lying.

Destiny is suspended. Death does not yet know on whom to pounce.

SEVENTEEN

Lithe and slim, Ammal and Myriam advance in this blaze of yellow material. They want to be indistinguishable, so have covered their hair with headscarves of the same colour. Each is holding a long, silky scarf.

Kalya holds her breath, she will not take her eyes off them.

Without hurrying, without looking round, the young women advance towards the centre of the square. Fever surges through their limbs, causes their hearts to tremble.

*

Wearing a white tunic with a red belt, Slimane comes into the room and invites Kalya to join Odette for breakfast.

She leaves the window and walks towards him.

'Thank you, Slimane. I'll come later.'

The Sudanese servant carries in his heart all the understanding in the world. His greying hair under his richly coloured skullcap, his caring face and his eyes, misty with gentleness, are a soothing sight.

He points to Sybil's room.

'I can hear her moving about. Shall I call her?'

'Later.'

Kalya will call her herself when it is all over. Why had she thought 'over'? She corrected herself: 'When it all begins.' She and Sybil will go everywhere together in this town which they already loved, which was already engraved in their flesh. Hand in hand, before parting, they will walk together one last time. Then, each of them will board the plane that will take them back to their separate countries, but they will come back another year: a promise they will make before taking off.

Slimane went out again. Kalya watched him close the door behind him as he left. She noticed a poor repair in the hem of his spotless white tunic, a different piece of material, a brighter red, sewn on to the back of his frayed belt, and because of this she would remember that exit very clearly. Slimane made a large contribution to the appearances that Odette managed to keep up, despite the modesty of her present means.

*

After Slimane's departure, just as Kalya was calmly walking back over to the window, she thought she heard a dull bang. But she did not pay any attention to it.

In the square, however, the die was cast.

Kalya leaned out of the window as far as she could.

The two young women were on the ground. One of them lay motionless on her back, bleeding. The other lay straddled over her. She sat up then bent over her again.

Speechless, petrified, Kalya refused to accept it.

A few moments later, she crossed the living room and rushed towards the door. From the depths of her armchair, Odette called her back, quickly removing her earplugs:

'What's happening? Where are you going?'

Kalya shouted a few words and continued on her way. Surprised by this change of plan, Slimane followed her as far as the hall. There, she took something hidden from the chest of drawers. Her movement was so rapid that he did not have time to glimpse the revolver.

Leaning over the stairwell, the Sudanese watched her go down.

'What's happened? An accident? I'm coming.'

Without stopping, she shouted:

'No, no. Stay there, Slimane. Don't leave Odette, or the child!'

Shortly afterwards, Sybil, barefoot, and in her pyjamas, arrived on the landing.

Kalya was deafened by the sound of her own footsteps on the stairs, by the throbbing of her temples. She reproached herself for having taken her eyes off the square for a few seconds, and did not hear the girl running behind her.

Odette heaved herself out of her armchair, looked for her slippers, gave up trying to find them, then, trembling, made her way over to the window. In the square, she recognized Myriam's yellow dress, which she had helped finish hemming. Although she didn't understand what was happening, she felt the burden of disaster crushing down and ran to the telephone to call the police, an ambulance and the fire brigade.

Never had Odette felt so alone. So alone. Where were the men in her life? Farid, Farid's strength? Mitry's tenderness? If only Mario were there to comfort her! He was still looking for his son, and had not been seen for the last forty-eight hours. The next door neighbours were still on vacation; a long, long way away, in Europe, America...

*

Now that the child had left the apartment, Slimane wondered who he was supposed to stay with. Which one should he protect? The old lady or the child?

He glanced at Odette. She was flapping about like a moth bumping into the lights, running hither and thither. He looked at the display cabinets for a few seconds, that mountain of objects and memories, and thought about their universe which was falling apart.

He thought about the little girl who had come from so far away and who would soon be leaving for new worlds, and suddenly he feared a risk, a danger which he sensed without understanding. At once, he decided to join her.

'The child is in the street. I'll run after her and bring her back.'

'Quickly Slimane, don't leave me on my own too long.'

A shot had broken the silence. A dull sound, covered by a further blanket of silence. A single shot. A few seconds' inattention and everything had been overturned.

Kalya moves forward through this grim silence, through this void. Walls, doors and shutters remain closed. She moves forward through this nowhere land, like others that have seen disaster grow and spread.

Nothing but a square. Nothing but a stretch of asphalt. Nothing but a killer, still lying in wait perhaps. A killer without a motive? A fanatic from whichever side? Nothing moves. Except Kalya's white dress, an ideal target for a marksman.

A line stretches from the apartment block to the centre of the square, a furrow from Sybil to Myriam and Ammal, a conductor of life. Time is suspended A truce, under siege from questions, weighed down with memories.

The narrow hand of time closes around lives, then deposits them in the same dust. Why bring to an end this spark across the abyss, why forestall the act of death? How to pull up those roots which separate and divide when they should enrich the song of everybody with their vigour? What makes up the flesh of man, the texture of his soul, the impenetrability of his heart? Beneath so many words, actions, layers, where does life breathe?

*

Kalya is arriving. Kalya approaches. A few seconds more.

The hidden killer did not fire one bullet more. The young

woman sitting up is no longer frantic. She calms down, she is waiting for help to come. Perhaps the other one is only slightly wounded?

The windows will open, the ambulance will arrive. Everything has not yet been said...

EIGHTEEN

Before Odette's telephone call, one of the lookouts had already reported the accident. An ambulance, on duty in a neighbouring district, was on its way. The siren could be heard as the white vehicle reached the square.

The nurses jumped out followed by five men carrying a stretcher and emergency equipment. They surrounded the two young women and moved back Kalya and the small gathering that had just formed. Someone shouted:

'Is it serious? Is she dead?'

At first, there was no reply. Then the chief went over to the crowd.

'Don't worry, she'll pull through.'

'What about all that blood?'

'She's only wounded.'

Kalya tried to get closer, so that Myriam and Ammal could see her, to say a few words to them.

'Come to the hospital tomorrow. She has lost a lot of blood but she'll be all right.'

Kalya still did not know which of the two had been hit but it did not make much difference. Injured together, they would recover together, bound closer together and more determined than ever. The nurses were all around them; they carried them to the ambulance. Before it drove off, a young doctor shouted to the crowd:

'Go home. Everything will be all right.'

The more anxious continued to gather around the pool of blood beside which lay a yellow scarf.

*

A breeze arose. The forgotten scarf fluttered over the square. Then it blew around, sometimes quickly, sometimes slowly, unfurling its radiant colour.

Kalya tried to get rid of her gun, glad not to have used it. A feeling of peace, of trust, of indescribable happiness surged up in her. She walked over to the edge of the square, emptied the magazine, and stuffed the bullets in her pocket, intending to get rid of them later. She threw the revolver away.

Turning around towards the square, she recognized the scarf. It shimmered, billowed and waved about, blown by the breeze. Kalya thought of retrieving it to give it back to one of the two young women. It would be useful next time. Nothing had been lost.

*

In the porchway, Sybil was waving excitedly to her. Slimane was standing behind her. He had brought the tortoise which he found wandering about on the landing.

Kalya looked from one image to the other: from the diaphanous scarf to the small blonde girl, then to the peaceful face of the Sudanese. She shouted:

'Everything's all right. Everything's all right!'

Then, she made her way back to the gutter, anxious to get rid of those lead bullets as soon as possible.

XIV

'Do you realize, Kalya, what Fred wanted to give me? A gun. Me! Can you imagine your grandmother holding a gun? Your uncle's off his head! Sometimes I think he really is mad.'

We had arrived at the door of her hotel room. Nouza threw it open, still laughing. The sight which greeted her left her speechless.

In front of the three-sided mirror, Anaïs had slipped into one of my grandmother's dresses, though she had trouble doing it up.

She lost her composure. The powder puff she was holding fell to the floor. She burst into tears. Nouza did not know what to say. I took her hand.

'That pink suits her much better than it does you, Grandma.'

She was not offended and took advantage of my comment to reverse the situation.

'You see, Anaïs, my own granddaughter thinks this dress looks better on you than it does on me. I'm sure she's right.'

Choking through her tears, Anaïs protested, shaking her head over and over.

'I often overdo it, don't contradict me. I curl my hair, I wear perfume, make-up, I choose fashionable clothes. All that to deceive time. But old age has come. It's here, well and truly here. Keep the dress.'

*

For some time, Anaïs had been neglecting her duties. She became upset at the slightest thing.

Nouza suspected that a love affair had disrupted her maid's all

146

too monotonous existence. She was moved by this and tried to make things easier for her. At the same time she felt a profound sadness, as if she sensed that it was too late for Anaïs and that her very innocence condemned her. She did not dare speak to her about it.

Anaïs picked up the powder puff, wrapped herself in her housecoat and turning to my grandmother, said:

'Shall I make you a coffee?'

'No, thank you.'

Then calling on me as a witness:

'Do you know, Anaïs, what my brother Farid wanted to give me? Guess! Kalya was there.'

'I don't know.'

'A revolver!'

'A revolver?'

'Because of what happened last year, at the neighbours. Do you remember that murder?'

Anaïs shivered and turned pale.

'I'll never be able to forget it.'

'If burglars broke into my house, I wouldn't shout. I'd pretend to be asleep, I'd snore. Or I'd say to them: "I'll give you everything. Take it all, I haven't seen you. But let me live." '

Anaïs nodded in agreement:

'Life is the main thing. Life...'

*

She recalled the murder. The whole neighbourhood, the whole town had been shaken by it.

Anaïs still shook at the thought of it. She knew Vittorio, hand-some, so elegant in his navy blue uniform with his stiff peaked cap on his head. He would sometimes come to ask a favour and she found him very attractive. But nobody found Anaïs attractive. Particularly not Vittorio. He only had eyes for fancy women, women in furs and jewels, with too much make-up. She caught sight of him in their company. Was he their pimp, she wondered.

*

That same evening, Anaïs unpicked the darts in the pink dress. She wore it to meet Henri. The young man had been her lover for a week.

NINETEEN

At the precise moment when Kalya leaned into the gutter and threw the bullets down the drain, she heard:

'Kalya! Kalya! Can I come now? I'm coming!'

The child did not give her a chance to reply. Escaping Slimane's guard, she rushed into the square.

Rooted to the spot, all Kalya could do was watch her run.

*

The child raced towards her, crowned by her glistening shock of hair.

She ran barefoot, the scarf almost made her trip. She freed herself with one bound and ran even faster. Her long hair spread out around her in a pale, floating mass, evoking thatch, corn, spring.

Sybil ran at top speed. Ran even faster.

At times, she looked as though she were flying, as if her feet would never touch the ground again.

Behind her, Slimane had sprung into action.

It was too late to call the little girl back, take her back inside. The danger was over, dawn was sweeping into every nook and cranny of the square. The child was still shouting:

'I'm coming! I'm here!'

Kalya had one knee on the ground and was kneeling, still, ready to receive her in her open arms.

XV

From every shadowy recess, from every summer shore, from the depths of all sadness, from the brink of every smile, from the edges of absence, from every desert, from every sky, Nouza appears, forever, at the crossroads in my life, her arms open, to receive me.

*

When I enter the gaming room, my grandmother sits up, drops her cards and, at the risk of losing the game, kisses me: 'I missed you, Kalya. What a good idea it was to come.'

*

Sometimes on Sunday, when I leave the boarding school and her car, driven by Omar, comes to fetch me, I slide back the sunroof, stand up on the seat and look at the city of Cairo, despite Anaïs's protests:

'You're swallowing all the dust. You'll make yourself ill!'

The avenue stretches out far from the mysterious narrow streets which I can make out behind us but which Omar will never drive down. We drive alongside the tram coming up from Heliopolis with its load of passengers; their bodies spill out of the doors and windows and congregate on the roof.

Further on, we reach the Place de la Gare, jammed with motor cars, donkey carts and hand-carts. A procession of camels threads its way through the crowds of pedestrians. The jerky movements of the policeman, dressed in white, suddenly cease. He lowers his arms and gives up directing the traffic. He removes his red fez and mops his forehead and neck, cursing.

I read the time on the Big Clock, it is still a long time till lunch at my grandmother's, where I am invited once a month. I recognize the 'departure hall', its constant coming and going. Nouza and I have crossed it five times together, when we went on vacation to Alexandria, to Lebanon or to other countries far away.

We drive alongside the Nile. Leaning out of the window, I sit and look at it and the feluccas going up and down. I feast my eyes on it, repeating to myself that it is the 'river of rivers', promise myself to remember it through all the landscapes of my life.

Anaïs and Omar then take me for a walk in the garden of the Grottoes, with its aquariums and rockeries; or to the zoological gardens.

After we had visited the hippopotamus nicknamed Sayeda Eshta, the Cream Lady, whose bulbous body, in contrast to her tiny eyes and fine ears, delighted me, I would go over to the orang-utang's cage.

I could watch him for hours. His eyes gaze at me with the utmost melancholy, I never walk away from this confrontation unscathed. I feel as if the animal is trying to communicate through speech which is cruelly imprisoned within his body and that, if I were really attentive, it would get through to me.

*

A group of children, full of joy and mockery, crowds round the motor car, running their grubby hands across its gleaming wings which Omar polishes and shines every morning with his chamois leather.

They greet us with applause, then beg for money. One of them waves to me through the windscreen, another plays with the wipers, a third makes faces in the mirror. The little girls amuse themselves by strutting up and down and laughing at their reflections in the hub caps.

With flicks of the fly swat, Omar sends them scarpering in all directions. I try in vain to restrain his arm. Anaïs hustles me into the car.

Feeling ill-at-ease, I sit awkwardly on the edge of the seat. A lame boy with one eye taps on the window. One hand offers me a dahlia, he holds out the other:

'Baksheesh!'

I have no handbag, my pockets are empty. Not even a sweet.

'Give. Give him something, Anaïs.'

'Why him and not the others? There'll be squabbles the minute we've left.'

The car drives off.

Shortly afterwards, we enter the residential district, far from the hubbub and squalor of the huge city, which shudders, swarms and struggles in the distance.

*

Laden with thoughts that are too much to bear, I run to Nouza and snuggle up to her silky clothes.

'If only you knew, Grandma.'

'I know, I know. But what can we do?'

'If you could have seen...'

'One would have to devote one's whole life, do you hear, one's whole life. Otherwise, what is the use? A drop in the ocean! Talk to your grandfather Nicolas about it.'

*

With all my six years, with all my seven years, with all my nine, ten, twelve years, I ran to Nouza. Nouza who always welcomed me, and showered me with presents every birthday.

Affectionate, stubborn Nouza, so light and so strong. My capricious and frivolous grandmother, fiery and indomitable. My fresh, my free Nouza. My river, my rock.

TWENTY

Mario had just parked his car in a nearby underground garage and was preparing to return home. After a crazy, three-day venture, he had finally secured Georges' release. The latter was to join him later that morning.

He left the garage, saw the ambulance go past, and had no idea that his daughter, Myriam, was inside.

Coming out into the square, he was astonished to see Kalya, by the gutter, leaning forward, her arms outstretched. At the same time, he saw Sybil running at full speed towards her. What were they doing out at this hour? What game were they playing?

And Slimane, with his tall erect figure? Why was he walking so slowly?

'I've found Georges!'

Mario shouts at him, then at her. Have they heard him? They have eyes only for the little girl who is running as fast as her legs will carry her.

He is captivated by the sight, too. Mario derives such pleasure from watching this beautiful child, from admiring her long strides, the lightness of her arms, the vitality of her body, the flow of her hair, that he does not hear the dull whistle of the bullet. Caught in mid-flight, it has just hit her between the shoulders.

Sybil continues running, as though she has not noticed it.

She runs. She goes on for a few seconds. Then she collapses. Suddenly.

*

The Sudanese rushes over. In his haste, the tortoise slips out of his hands, falls on its back and bounces several times on the ground.

Slimane has just reached the child. He kneels down, picks her up and regaining all his strength, stands up carrying her in his arms. Standing up, blind to everything around him, he looks up towards the heavens, beseeching. Suddenly, unable to control himself any longer, he begins to spin, to whirl round on the spot. Faster and faster, like a dancing dervish. Gripped by this fever, he turns, turns, unable to stop.

A lullaby, from the recesses of his childhood and the lands of the Nile, pierces sorrows and mists, and rises to his lips. Only then does he slow down. One twirl after another, slower and slower.

Slimane's words mingle with those of the old song. His words link the history of the river – with its ditches, its torrents, its delta – to that of life and its many mysteries. The Sudanese's voice chokes, breaks; then, gradually, swells:

> Water goes water comes
> Upstream downstream
> Carrying away the springs
> and the mouths of night
>
> Speaking of marshes
> Stirring up suns and sands
> Brimming with new floods
> Devouring the breath of the seas
>
> Upstream downstream
> Water goes water comes
> As parched as hunger
> And gentler than the heart.

Slimane is no longer moving. He is very calm, absorbed by his tune.

Slimane sings for the peaceful child who looks as though she is sleeping. This child from far away. From far, so far away. Like him...

A hail of buckshot riddled him now, interrupting the song.

Once more, silence.

Kalya has reached the end of her journey. Her heart no longer knows what to hold on to, one after the other her muscles give way. She slowly collapses. On the ground, she is nothing but an inert mass.

A few seconds ago, her arms open to receive Sybil, she saw the child hit, stopped in mid-flight. A fatal, irreversible moment, that suddenly blotted out her own life. Her vigour and strength abandon her. She does not struggle, no longer wants this breath lingering on the edge of her lips.

Everything happens very quickly. Mario, he does not know how, suddenly finds himself there, kneeling at Kalya's side, trying to make himself heard: 'I've found Georges. Everything's settled.'

He persists. He lies. He hopes his words will reach her:

'Sybil will fly out tomorrow. Everything's settled. Everything's settled.'

'Everything's settled' echoes, rings incessantly in her ears. Kalya would like to shake her head, but the words persist. They mingle with 'I'll find you again one day,' with other words spoken, with those of Slimane and Sybil, who sang together: 'The water goes the water comes.'

Nouza's smile tries to break through the mists.

*

Men, women, rush into the square. Shutters open. Doors open. Cries, shouts rise up all around; this indiscriminate violence cannot, will not last.

Tomorrow, the apocalypse, a sea of madness? Tomorrow, peace?

A little boy, who saw it all, looks at the square and the people there. In his mind, things have begun to stir.

*

The yellow scarf, stained with blood, flaps in the breeze. It retains in its folds the tenacious brightness of the morning.

The piece of cloth rises, billows, falls, rises again, takes off, flutters; falls once more then flies off, even higher...

Also published by Serpent's Tail

From Sleep Unbound
Andrée Chedid

'Andrée Chedid tells this story as though she were a jeweller assembling a bomb; her precision and grace (and those of her translator) are remorseless.'

HARRIETT GILBERT

'*From Sleep Unbound* captures not one woman's world, but that of *all* women, whether . . . cloistered and closeted in a society bound by retrograde customs or in a modern metropolis, liberated for all intents and purposes, but imprisoned within their own psychological cells.' BETTINA KNAPP

'A brilliant, touching book.'

VICTORIA BRITTAIN, *The Guardian*

'A passionate study of life imprisonment.'

JENNY DISKI, *New Statesman*

'Chedid's spare but beautiful prose makes of this uneventful life a moving parable of oppression and the human spirit's capacity to fight it.' *7 Days*

'A deep, poetic meticulous exploration of the mind and history of . . . a woman who liberates herself by killing the husband who has tyrannized her.' *TLS*

'Chedid's beautiful tale is a timely reminder that the freedoms Western women take for granted concern them alone.' *City Limits*

160 pages £4.95 (paper)

Beer in the Snooker Club
Waguih Ghali

'This is a wonderful book. Quiet, understated, seemingly without any artistic or formal pretensions. Yet quite devastating in its human and political insights . . . If you want to convey to someone what Egypt was like in the forties and fifties, and why it is impossible for Europeans or Americans to understand, give them this book. It makes *The Alexandria Quartet* look like the travel brochure it is.'

GABRIEL JOSIPOVICI

"One of the best novels about Egypt ever written. It is marvellously cheering that it is available again after twenty years.' AHDAF SOUEIF

'Written with honesty, warmth and humour, and makes compelling reading.' *Race & Class*

'Ghali is a superb stylist and creator of dialogue . . . and *Beer in the Snooker Club* a haunting statement of cultural alienation.'

CHRIS SEARLE, *Morning Star*

'Should be ranked . . . along with the best of Naguib Mahfouz. As sharp and relevant today as when it was first published, and its reappearance is, therefore, most welcome.' *Literary Review*

'A comic masterpiece.' *The Observer*

'An excellent novel.' *The Guardian*

224 pages £5.95 (paper)

Also published by Serpent's Tail

The Lonely Hearts Club
Raul Nuñez

'Magnificent.' *Blitz*

'The singles scene of Barcelona's lonely low life. Sweet and seedy.' *Elle*

'A celebration of the wit and squalor of Barcelona's mean streets.' *City Limits*

'This tough and funny story of low life in Barcelona manages to convey the immense charm of that city without once mentioning Gaudi. . . . A story of striking freshness, all the fresher for being so casually conveyed.' *The Independent*

'A sardonic view of human relations . . .'
The Guardian

'Threatens to do for Barcelona what *No Mean City* once did for Glasgow.' *Glasgow Herald*

'A funny low life novel of Barcelona.' *The Times*

160 pages £6.95 (paper)

Landscapes After the Battle
Juan Goytisolo

'Juan Goytisolo is one of the most rigorous and original contemporary writers. His books are a strange mixture of pitiless autobiography, the debunking of mythologies and conformist fetishes, passionate exploration of the periphery of the West – in particular of the Arab world which he knows intimately – and audacious linguistic experiment. All these qualities feature in *Landscapes After the Battle*, an unsettling, apocalyptic work, splendidly translated by Helen Lane.'   MARIO VARGAS LLOSA

'*Landscapes After the Battle* . . . a cratered terrain littered with obscenities and linguistic violence, an assault on "good taste" and the reader's notions of what a novel should be.'   *The Observer*

'Fierce, highly unpleasant and very funny.'
The Guardian

'A short, exhilarating tour of the emergence of pop culture, sexual liberation and ethnic militancy.'
New Statesman

'Helen Lane's rendering reads beautifully, capturing the whimsicality and rhythms of the Spanish without sacrificing accuracy, but rightly branching out where literal translation simply does not work.'
Times Literary Supplement

176 pages £7.95 (paper)

Marks of Identity
Juan Goytisolo

'For me *Marks of Identity* was my first novel. It was forbidden publication in Spain. For twelve years after that everything I wrote was forbidden in Spain. So I realized that my decision to attack the Spanish language through its culture was correct. But what was most important for me was that I no longer exercised censorship on myself, I was a free writer. This search for and conquest of freedom was the most important thing to me.'

Juan Goytisolo, in an interview with *City Limits*

'Juan Goytisolo is by some distance the most important living novelist from Spain ... and *Marks of Identity* is undoubtedly his most important novel, some would say the most significant work by a Spanish writer since 1939, a truly historic milestone.'

The Guardian

'A masterpiece which should whet the appetites of British readers for the rest of the trilogy.'

Times Literary Supplement

352 pages £8.95 (paper)

The Devil's Trill
Daniel Moyano

'The first English publication, in superb translation, of one of Argentina's finest writers (in exile). Moyano, like his hero Triclinio, finds harmonies in discord and, playing ironic accompaniment to the Devil's tunes, brings music out of madness.... With fine wit and artistry, Moyano has written a political parable that movingly sings the triumph of the human spirit.'
Sunday Times

'Daniel Moyano is a superb writer.... The absence of an English translation of his writing is one of those literary lapses one reads about as happening to other places and other ages.' ANDREW GRAHAM-YOOLL

'An eloquent defence of artistic integrity and freedom ... the book is a real triumph.' JOHN KING

'Daniel Moyano's deep realism blends both modern and classical prose, progressive thought and a profound faith in the ability of human beings to suvive.' RAFAEL CONTE

128 pages £6.50 (paper)

The Lizard's Tail
Luisa Valenzuela

'Luisa Valenzuela has written a wonderfully free ingenious novel about sensuality and power and death, the "I" and literature. Only a Latin American could have written *The Lizard's Tail*, but there is nothing like it in contemporary Latin American literature.' SUSAN SONTAG

'By knotting together the writer's and the subject's fates, Valenzuela creates an extraordinary novel whose thematic ferocity and baroque images explore a political situation too exotically appalling for reportage.' *The Observer*

'Its exotic, erotic forces seduce with consummate, subliminal force.' *Blitz*

'Don't classify it as another wonder of "magic realism": read, learn and fear.' *Time Out*

'*The Lizard's Tail* will probably sell far fewer copies than Isabel Allende's inferior *Of Love and Shadows*, and that is a great pity. [It] is a wild adventurous book . . . a gripping and challenging read.'

Third World Quarterly

288 pages £7.95 (paper)

Also published by Serpent's Tail

Dreaming of Dead People
Rosalind Belben

This is an intimate portrait of a woman approaching middle-age, lonely, starved of love, yet avoiding the seductions of resentment. First published ten years ago and now reissued in paperback by Serpent's Tail, *Dreaming of Dead People* is a joyful, stark novel by one of the most distinctive voices of contemporary fiction.

'Rosalind Belben's eye for the movement and texture of the natural world is extraordinarily acute and she has a poet's ear for language. Her book, although apparently a cry of loneliness and deprivation, is also a confession of fulfilment, of endless curiosity for, and love of, life.' SELINA HASTINGS, *Daily Telegraph*

'[Belben's] heroine is a solitary woman who is suffering as she reconciles herself to loneliness and sterility. She tells of her past and recalls, often, the countryside, where being alone is not painful and, if there is no meaning to life, the call to the senses is immediate.' HILARY BAILEY,*The Guardian*

'So extraordinarily good that one wants more, recognizing a writer who can conjure an inner life and spirit, can envisage, in unconnected episodes, a complete world: one unified not by external circumstances but by patterns of the writer's mind.'
ISABEL QUIGLY, *Financial Times*

160 pages £6.95 (paper)